THE NEW SINGAPORE HORROR COLLECTION

THE NEW SINGAPORE HORROR COLLECTION

S.J. Huang

 Marshall Cavendish
Editions

With the support of

NATIONAL ARTS COUNCIL
SINGAPORE

Published by Marshall Cavendish Editions
An imprint of Marshall Cavendish International

A member of the
Times Publishing Group

Other Marshall Cavendish Offices: Marshall Cavendish Corporation, 99 White
Plains Road, Tarrytown NY 10591-9001, USA • Marshall Cavendish International
(Thailand) Co Ltd, 253 Asoke, 12th Flr, Sukhumvit 21 Road, Klongtoey Nua,
Wattana, Bangkok 10110, Thailand • Marshall Cavendish (Malaysia) Sdn Bhd, Times
Subang, Lot 46, Subang Hi-Tech Industrial Park, Batu Tiga, 40000 Shah Alam,
Selangor Darul Ehsan, Malaysia.

National Library Board, Singapore Cataloguing-in-Publication Data

Name: Ng, Shuojie.
Title: The new Singapore horror collection / S. J. Huang.
Description: Singapore : Marshall Cavendish, [2019]
Identifier(s): OCN 1120753073 | ISBN 978-981-48-6822-8 (paperback)
Subject(s): LCSH: Horror tales, English--Singapore. | Ghost stories, Singaporean
(English)
Classification: DDC S823--dc23

Printed in Singapore

For Wei Xuan,
my light and star

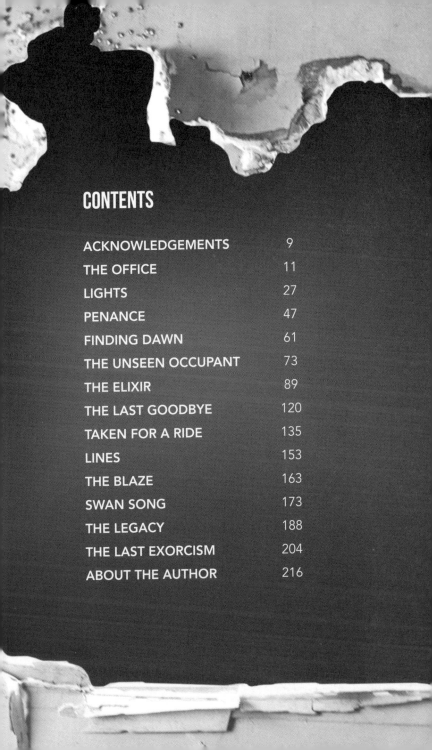

CONTENTS

ACKNOWLEDGEMENTS

First off, to all the wonderful folks at Marshall Cavendish: Anita Teo, She-reen Wong, Mindy Pang and Lo Yi Min, thank you for being so patient throughout the whole process and making my first publication experience such a breeze.

To Nicky Moey, one of my favourite horror authors—a special thank you for reading my work and your kind words on the cover. I am immensely honoured.

To my cousin Qi Yang, thank you for gamely reading all the stories I sent you. Your encouragement kept me going.

To Mom and Dad, thank you for your love and support, and for always pushing me to do my best.

And most of all to my girlfriend, Wei Xuan—thank you for being my editor, critic and biggest fan. You believed in me and my work when I didn't. There would have been no book without you.

THE OFFICE

When finally his colleagues were all done with their congratulations, Jimmy found himself alone in his cubicle once more. The office was fast emptying—it was a Friday, after all—but he took his time to tidy the scattered files and papers on his desk. What he was about to do happened only a few times in one's career, if one was even that lucky, and he wanted to savour every moment.

"Not going yet?" Aaron, on his way out, paused to look at him.

"Nope. Got plenty to tidy, plenty to move."

His colleague laughed. "You don't have to do it today, you know? Your new office isn't going to run away."

Jimmy returned a chuckle. "I know, I know. Just want to get it sorted out so I can hit the ground running next week."

"And that's why they promoted you. See ya."

From his desk he could hear the *ding!* as the lift arrived. The office became deathly quiet.

For about two hours he worked in complete silence, oblivious to the dying light outside the windows. Done at last, he regarded his handiwork. At least half a dozen stacks of papers and folders, rising neatly like the skyscrapers shining in the dark outside, ready to be carried to the next phase of his career. He cast his eye at the window, taking in the jewelled towers glittering beyond. Once, a long time ago, he had stood at the feet of these behemoths, staring up in wonder, feeling an insatiable hunger stirring within him. To be at the top, no matter what it took.

And here he was. He stood up, looking over the cubicle wall into the dark, empty room awaiting him. Now that the moment was here, it felt strangely anti-climactic. No cheers, no applause. Just him and his things, and he even had to move them himself. After all the things he had to do to get to this point…all he felt now was fatigue and a faint impatience to get it over and done with.

His phone buzzed. A WhatsApp message from Aaron.

My god, did you see the news?

He scrolled further.

"Man Falls to His Death…" read a link to the *Straits Times* website.

For a blank moment he wondered why Aaron had sent him that, only to feel his throat tightening as the first tendrils of suspicion clenched his gut. His thumb hovered over the link uncertainly. It *couldn't* be. Why on earth would Chris even…

He felt a chilly wind in his face and a shaky weakness in his legs. All at once he was staring down from a great, dizzying height at the narrow strips of road hardly thicker than his shoelaces, and specks of people and cars so far away they moved with indifferent muteness. Jimmy shook his head, but the mental image clung on stubbornly. He could feel the strong gusts buffeting him from behind, egging him on. One foot already lifted, a ridiculously shined oxford trembling in thin air. One step forward, and it would all—

He sat down quickly, feeling his strength forsake him utterly.

He had to know.

His thumb jabbed the screen so hard he could hear the clack of thumbnail against hard glass. A white screen, a dawdling blue line slowly crawling right. The page took forever to load.

SINGAPORE: A man was seen falling to his death from an office tower in the CBD on Friday evening, in full view of passers-by below. Witnesses say the man, wearing a mustard yellow dress shirt and black pants, appeared to have fallen from Sky Plaza.

No. No. *Breathe*, Jimmy told himself. *You've got to breathe.*

I think it's Chris man, Aaron went on relentlessly. *Mustard yellow, his fav colour. Remb what he said when they fired him? I will jump. I will jump in front of all of you. Sky plaza is just opp, maybe you can—*

Fuck this! Jimmy threw down his phone. He could hear his own ragged breathing. For a while he stared blankly into the air, before a sudden impulse jerked his eyes upwards, forcing him to look upon the cold, lifeless room that was now his.

He felt his skin crawl.

No, not today. He had to leave. All his papers and things, piled on his table, waiting—they'd just have to stay where they were till Monday. He was getting out of there. He grabbed his jacket and laptop bag and made for the lift lobby.

The lift wouldn't come. Frantically, he slammed repeatedly at the call button, but it wouldn't light up. He looked up at the display above the lift.

Out of Service.

He ran—he didn't know why he had to run, but he did—to the stairwell, feeling a rush of relief as he found the door unlocked. But as he stared over the railings, seeing how the steps spiralled down endlessly in neat, cascading rectangles, his spirits sank. Sixty-six storeys. There had to be another way.

He would call for help. Somewhere in his phone, somewhere, he had the number to the maintenance office. All he had to do was give them a call, and they would sort it out. They had to.

He returned to the lift lobby and dialled their number, but there was no reception. He waved his phone around and waited for a bit, tapping his feet. He knew the building had decent coverage. As the minutes trickled by and nothing changed, he began to feel cold all over. It couldn't all be coincidence, the lifts not working, and now his phone. He paced about at the lobby, reluctant to go back to his desk. He didn't want to see the dark, empty room staring back at him so accusingly. The room had once belonged to Chris and now it seemed to glare at Jimmy like an empty eye socket, gouged of life.

"My god, I'm being ridiculous." He felt a little better hearing his own voice, even if it echoed slightly in the still emptiness. "You know what, I'll just send the bloody fellows at the maintenance office an email. They better still be around. Or heads will roll."

He strode back to his cubicle, averting his eyes so that he wouldn't have to see the vacant office, but it remained at the periphery of his vision, shadowed and sinister.

He booted up his laptop and sent the email. Within minutes he had a reply.

Hi Mr Ang,
To my knowledge the lifts are currently operational.

Allow me to check if everything is in order, and I'll get back to you.

"Great, just great. Bunch of incompetent idiots." He leaned back into his chair, rubbing his tired eyes. He could kill for a nice cold beer.

His heart stopped cold. The lights in Chris's office were on.

He felt his eyes squeeze shut and his head dipping, almost as if bracing for a blow. *Breathe, breathe.* Steeling himself, he slowly opened his eyes to where he thought his laptop screen to be, squinting laboriously so that all was shut out save for the small rectangle of light right in front of him. Every breath came out in quivering starts. *Please, please, come on.*

One new email.

Hi Mr Ang,
The lifts are working fine. Would you like to try again?

His shaking fingers set to work. *I cant call the lift wehre I am. Cld you please take the lift up to 66 flr?*

An agonising minute. Then, *Okay, give me a moment.*

Hurry, you idiot, he begged silently, his head still bowed, huddling over the laptop like a caveman over life-giving fire. His neck was starting to hurt. *Hurry, hurry.*

The still silence of the office was now close to suffocating. He squeezed his eyes shut, so hard that stars spat and sputtered in the inky blackness. Every hair on his being stood erect, tingling antennas afraid to receive. With each rustle of an errant sheaf or creak of a roguish table, he gave an agonised twitch and sank deeper into a foetal position. In the grey, buzzing waters of his mind there was a single pinprick of light—the *ding!* of the lift that would spell salvation.

A whimper escaped him. He could hear the murmur of feet dragging themselves across the carpet. No, there was no mistake. Closing his eyes had only made his hearing all the more acute. The sound seemed to have started from Chris's room and was approaching his cubicle—any moment now, if he raised his head, he would see Chris peering over his cubicle wall with those disapproving eyes of his, as he always did back when he was still the boss. Before *he* had gotten him fired.

"No...*please.*" The words were drawn from him as they would from a child facing the rod, a prisoner facing the noose. "*Please...*"

The shuffling stopped—awfully close to his cubicle. He felt a twinge in his bladder. As the seconds crept by and the silence continued, unbroken, a part of him began to reel from the sheer fatigue of terror. *Look up*, a voice in his mind whispered. *Just look up and it will be over.*

He opened his eyes. The carpet at his feet swam in and out of focus, streaked with flashes of black. Too much blood in his head. As his vision began to clear, the mundane, ordinary sight of his shoes set against the carpet began to make him feel foolish. There were no unusual sounds, no shuffling to be heard. Even his shallow, panicked breathing was starting to slow. He had allowed his mind to play tricks on him.

Then right above him, someone—*something* cleared its throat.

He screamed. He shot up and tore to the lobby, his fear-cramped thighs screeching in protest. Once there he could barely stand; his legs were wobbling so badly. Palms on knees, he took a deep breath. Then another. And another. The voice of reason bubbled up in his consciousness. He hadn't seen anything as he leapt up. Nothing. No one, nothing, not even a shadow. Just the lights in Chris's room. He was being ridiculous. Completely ridiculous.

It's just your bloody conscience, he told himself. *It's in overdrive.*

He hadn't meant anyone any harm, of course. But Chris had royally screwed up—why shouldn't he capitalise on it? It would've been stupid not to.

Anyone else in his place would have done the same, even Chris. *Especially* Chris.

Well, that idiot was gone. Crumbled like a soft little snowflake, crying and making all those silly threats when they fired him. *He had no right to do that*, Jimmy thought fiercely. *He knew how the game was played, he played the game himself. He had no right at all.* The heat of indignation melted the iciness in his chest, and his breathing settled into a tamer rhythm.

Now, where the hell was the maintenance person?

He jumped when the phone rang. It wasn't his mobile, but his office line. Or at least it sounded like it. He couldn't be sure, standing so far from his desk. Reluctantly he considered the dark path in front of him that led back to his cubicle. It was clear. No ghosts, no bogeyman. He craned his neck slightly forward to catch a glimpse of Chris's office. The lights were still on.

He cursed silently. That was the one thing he just couldn't account for. He could have sworn he hadn't set foot inside at all, much less turned on the lights. But…perhaps he had done so when he was preoccupied with the moving. "In the zone", so to speak. After all, he did like to know the lie of the land before he proceeded, and the re-location to the VP's office was as significant as any other project he had embarked on in his career. It was only natural for him to have gone into the room at some point to get a feel of the place, even if he hadn't consciously thought about it. All too natural.

In slow, mincing steps he started for his cubicle. As soon as the dreaded room came into sight he turned his eyes to meet it head-on, unblinking, almost daring it to do its worst. His steps became strides. The phone was still ringing when he arrived at his cubicle.

"Hello."

"Ah hi, Mr Ang. This is the maintenance office. I tried going up to the sixty-sixth floor but the lift just wouldn't stop there. Might be a technical fault."

"This is ridiculous, man. Can you get it fixed quickly, before I make a complaint?"

"I'm really sorry, sir, but I don't think it's something we can fix immediately. How about you come down to the sixty-fifth floor and try there?"

Jimmy made a cluck of irritation. "Cannot lah. My pass won't work on that floor." The building's security protocol required an access card to be tapped whenever one exited the stairwell to enter the office area. The sixty-fifth floor housed a different company, and his access card wasn't going to work on that floor.

"Don't worry, sir, I'll send one of my guys up to the sixty-fifth floor to open the stairwell door for you. Very sorry for the trouble, sir. But I think that's the only way you can get out for now."

"Seriously," he muttered as he hung up the phone. But it beat going down all sixty-six flights of stairs on foot.

His attention returned to Chris's—no, it was *his* room now—and taking a deep breath he strode inside and turned off the lights. It felt good. It felt normal. He was sane again.

The phone rang. He ran back to his desk and snatched up the receiver. "What now?"

Silence. Then a soft breathing filled his ear.

"Who's this?" he nearly shouted, his voice cracking.

The breathing stopped. "Why, Jimmy. Why."

He threw the receiver down and ran. He barged through the door to the stairwell and was on his way down to the sixty-third floor before he realised he had overshot. "Sixty-fifth floor," he muttered to himself. "He said sixty-fifth floor." Turning around reluctantly, he slowly trudged up the stairs. His heart was still thumping wildly and his breaths were staccato huffs. His shaking hand grasped blindly for the hand rail.

Just what the hell was that? The maintenance manager didn't seem like the kind who would dare play a stupid prank like that, but you never knew with people. That was the only explanation for it. He kicked the wall, more in frustration than fury. It was supposed to have been a day of celebration for him, a day of victory. Instead, he was running around like a dog with its tail between its legs. All because that idiot couldn't accept that he had lost, had chosen to kill himself like a freaking loser. Oh, and screw Aaron too, for telling him about it. What was he trying to imply?

Deep breaths, he told himself. Everything was under control. Nobody had seen his panicked outburst—and screw that prankster, whoever he was, he was going to pay for it—nobody saw him as anything other than the up-and-coming VP who was destined for great things. Everything was under control. Everything was okay.

He had reached the sixty-fifth floor landing. A tug at the door—locked. He tapped his access card. Denied, as expected. Where the hell was that guy? He shook the door by its handle, but it didn't budge.

"Hello!" he called. "I'm here!" Nothing. He peered through the narrow window in the door. A dim hallway leading to the lights of the lift lobby—empty. With a sigh he took a step back and folded his arms. *Five minutes*, he told himself. *Five more minutes and I'm going to walk down all the way to the fucking first floor and tear those idiots a new one.*

In the distance he thought he heard the *ding!* of the lift. Finally.

Footsteps echoed towards him from behind the closed door—and suddenly within him he felt a squeeze of primal fear. What if it wasn't the maintenance guy? He squinted through the window again. He could make out a silhouette, still fairly far off, coming towards him. Something, something was wrong. It looked…*familiar*, somehow. That wave of his hair, that saunter. The shape of his head.

His blood turned to ice. He knew that outline. How many times had that head popped up over the wall of his cubicle, demanding this, demanding that?

Oh god. No—it had to be mere coincidence. Many people with that type of hair, that shape of head. Common, very common. But in the little concrete enclosure that was the stairwell, he felt vulnerable. Nowhere to run but down, all sixty-plus floors of it. And horror of horrors—what if the exit on the ground floor was locked? He would be trapped with…whoever it was. What should he do?

He glanced at his watch—it was nearly 9 p.m. Ridiculous—he was being ridiculous again. He was meeting Mindy at 9.30 p.m., and she didn't like it when he was late. If he wanted any "dessert" after drinks tonight, he was going to have to man the hell up and grow a pair. Think of her, he told himself, think of her in that unbelievably tight dress. Those legs to die for, later to be enveloped in stockings, if he so wished.

He stole one more look at the approaching silhouette, this time a lot more cautiously. Closer up, and with a more collected mind, the sense of dread faded. He had been imagining things. But still he couldn't see the person's face. Just one glimpse, that was all he needed. There was a solitary bulb hanging midway in the corridor, and the shadowy figure was now nearly close enough for it to illuminate him.

A single point of light appeared, glinting, growing. The nose. Then the bridge of the nose, the turn of cheek. An eye—

All the roiling fear within nearly boiled over at the moment of revelation—he nearly screamed. It was all right, it was all right. He knew that guy. He had seen him mooching around the maintenance office more than once; that explained why he had found the outline and gait so familiar. Everything had a logical explanation. Everything.

He sighed with relief. He was going to be out of the damned place soon.

Someone tapped him on the shoulder, and instinctively he turned behind. The last thing he saw, before his slack jaw could even tighten into a scream, was a once-familiar face, mangled and bloodied, and a flash of mustard yellow, daubed with blood red.

—◠◠◠—

"So tell me," said the affable, portly man in his mid-50s, "what do you see?"

The younger man swallowed as he stared at what once had been a human being, as difficult as it was to believe it. "The…injuries look familiar, somehow."

The pathologist guffawed. "That is a major understatement. It looks exactly like the previous one we had."

"You mean the suicide? The one who jumped off some building in the CBD."

"Yep, all suicides from ten storeys up tend to be, shall we say, rather indistinguishable in appearance. But something's a little off here." He grabbed a clipboard from the surgical trolley and flipped through the sheaf of papers. "This one," he said, "was found by the maintenance officer in the stairwell of his office building. The lifts in the building were acting up, so the maintenance person went up to help the deceased. Said he heard a scuffle and a loud thud just before he opened the stairwell door for the deceased. Found the guy on the landing—and promptly fainted at the sight." He paused, his nose crinkling. He didn't like it when the facts didn't add up. He tossed the clipboard aside and returned his gaze to the cadaver before him. "You have to wonder what sort of scuffle would reduce someone to a veritable pulp."

"Maybe he was beaten up very badly. Someone bashed his head in and, um, the rest of his body to boot."

"Doesn't look like it at all. Not one bit. There would have been tell-tale marks, physical signs. No, this fella looks like he fell out of nowhere and met the landing with the force of a few hundred g's." He gave a sigh of resignation. "I'm sorry, Marcus, but I think this is going to be a long night for us."

The assistant nodded.

"Tell you something though," the pathologist said, his humour returning. "Don't think 'misadventure' is going to cut it here. The newspapers are going to have a field day when the coroner returns with his verdict."

The assistant looked at him expectantly.

"Death at the hands of person or persons unknown."

LIGHTS

Inspector David Chan was about to leave the station when he was forestalled by one of his colleagues.

"Someone's looking for you."

"*Now?*" The past thirty-six hours had been a blur—a particularly nasty murder had found its way to him—and at that moment there was nothing he wanted more than to take a hot shower and climb into bed.

"He says it's about the Orchid Secondary case."

Orchid Secondary. Orchid Secondary...

A thick sense of unease quickened in his gut a split-second before his brain thumbed the correct page. The incident about the schoolboy, still unsolved.

"That's nearly four months ago. Why's he coming in only now?"

Zach shrugged and turned to go. "Interview Room 1," he called over his shoulder. "Don't keep him waiting for long."

—◈—

Andy weaved his way through the heaps of jumbled clutter that dotted the field—a rash of opened cardboard boxes here, a pile of bright orange cones there, and white plastic bags everywhere fluttering festively in the wind. He made small detours around huddles of his fellow Scouts, some deep in conversation, some engrossed in work. To his relief, he saw that Tim was alone, so he strode up to where Tim was bending over a box, counting its contents.

"You sure this is a good idea?" Andy asked in a low voice.

"What?" Tim answered distractedly, and immediately his lips resumed their silent counting.

"The war games. *Your* special version of the war games this year."

The counting stopped, and Tim threw the bunch of light sticks in his hand back into the box. He looked at Andy and grinned.

"Someone's getting worried."

"I'm not. But"—Andy lowered his voice further—"you know what happened to Freddie."

"He ran away from home."

"That's what they're *guessing*. But people have been saying—"

"Yes, yes, we've all heard. You can't believe everything people say, you know?" Tim was shorter than Andy, but he had a habit of looking down his nose when speaking to others, a habit Andy found annoying as hell. Especially now.

"The *police* were here. Something was wrong." He glared at Tim. Ever since his friend became Troop Leader, he had been nothing but a pain in the butt. "You're just too freaking proud to admit that your stupid idea might not be so good after all."

"Well, *Mr Lim* didn't think it was a stupid idea." Again, that infuriating smug smile of his. "Just admit it—my idea is pretty awesome. What you're *really* worried about is getting thrashed tonight."

Andy rolled his eyes and threw a weak punch at him, but Tim simply laughed and danced out of reach.

"All right, all right, I'm kidding," Tim said, when he'd stopped laughing. "Come, help me count the light sticks. We need about thirty blue and thirty red for the war games."

Andy peered into the box. "I thought you were going to get green. Red and green."

"Bookshop auntie says she has no green ones. Supplier issues." A pause. "Tell you what, I'm gonna be nice and let you choose your team colour. Since, you know, I could win wearing red or blue, it doesn't really matter."

Andy picked up a bundle of light sticks bound by a thick elastic band, staring at the muted-red liquid within the un-activated light sticks. He hefted it in his hand for a moment, then carefully placed it back in the box. With a firm eye he met Tim's mirthful countenance, and his finger lanced forward to jab the smirking boy in the chest.

"Listen here, loser. My reds are going to stomp your blue ass tonight, buddy."

Tim's grin only grew wider.

———

"You're letting them play war games in the dark tonight? On the field?"

Mr Lim sighed. He had known it wouldn't be long before the inevitable question was asked. He turned from his marking to face his fellow teacher-in-charge.

"Yes. There's really no reason to say no."

"Aren't you worried about, you know…" Mr Tay stared at him hopefully, clearly reluctant to even give voice to his fear.

The senior teacher leaned back into his chair and folded his hands. "You heard what Principal said, Eric. He wants life in school to go on as usual."

The younger teacher nodded, but he remained hovering at the other's desk, his feet shuffling about irresolutely. "I'm just worried, you know? Parents nowadays, they're so difficult. If anything happens in the dark…"

"I know, I know. Truth be told, I'm a little worried too. But they'll be fine. We'll make sure of it."

"That whole…incident, it's *crazy*." Mr Tay shifted his weight from one foot to the other, his resolve not to wring his hands readily apparent from how his arms remained stiffly by his sides the whole time. "You saw the footage. We all saw the footage. There's no explanation for—"

"There's surely a logical explanation," Mr Lim cut in tersely, glancing around to see if anybody in the staffroom was close enough to overhear. "We just haven't found it yet."

As a teacher, there had been times Mr Lim was obliged to say things he himself didn't quite believe. And this was one of them. They had all seen the CCTV footage. *Studied* it, more like. For hours it had been put on repeat on nearly every screen in the staffroom. They'd examined it frame by frame, scrutinising it so closely that sometimes their noses rested on the screen. The police experts had examined it too. If there was a rational explanation for the whole thing, no one could see it.

Freddie had left the library at 7.30 p.m., when the library closed. Mrs Vishnu saw him leaving alone. It had been August then, so there were few students in the library to begin with. And the CCTVs outside the library corroborated what she said.

At 2 a.m. the police received a call from his frantic parents. He hadn't come home. And so the police came down to the school. Mr Lim was among the group of senior teachers called back to school by Principal. It was a surreal sight—the spinning blue and red lights, and the frenzy of activity in the dark of pre-dawn morning.

And the mystery only thickened from there on.

—◦◦◦—

"Mr Wong, right?"

The elderly man nodded. He shivered slightly in the thin button-down shirt that hung awkwardly on his gaunt frame. David searched for the air-con remote to turn up the temperature in Interview Room 1. It was kept cold by default. It encouraged the interviewees—the suspects, usually—to talk. But that wasn't necessary right now.

"You have something to tell me?" he asked.

"Y-yes."

"All right. Go ahead."

The man's Adam's apple bobbed as he swallowed, straining against the thin, wrinkled skin of his neck. He opened his mouth a few times, only to close it each time without a word. After this happened a few times, the detective stopped pacing about the room and took a seat opposite the man.

"Maybe it'll be easier if we start with what you told us previously," he said in Mandarin, flipping open a folder containing his notes.

The other man nodded mutely. David took a minute to study the papers.

"You're the caretaker-cum-security-guard at Orchid Secondary School. Earlier this year, on August 19th, from 6.15 p.m. to around midnight, you were on duty at your usual post, one of the side gates at the school that opens out to Burnley Road."

A nod. "That's correct, sir."

"At the school, all gates are to be closed and locked by six every evening, except for the side gate you're stationed at. Everyone entering or leaving the school after six is to go through that gate. On the evening in question, you locked all the other gates, as usual. You took your place at your post at about 6.15 p.m."

There had been a suspicion, at that time, that the caretaker had been guilty. Not of any crime, but dereliction of his duty and post. A smoke break, perhaps. Or simply dozing off. But he swore up and down that he hadn't left his post the whole time, not even for a single moment. And that he hadn't seen the boy leave. The CCTV above the side gate vindicated him. He had been there the entire time. And Freddie hadn't left through the gate.

"While you were on duty you noticed nothing suspicious. Then at midnight you locked the side gate and went to sleep in your bunk, which is a short distance away from the side gate."

David looked at the old man evenly. "Is there anything you'd like to add?"

The man's eyes, now large and earnest, stared at him most unsettlingly.

"Sir, there's something else."

David raised his eyebrows. "And why didn't you mention it the last time?"

The pair of frail, liver-spotted hands opposite him twisted and twiddled. He had seen such behaviour before in suspects and witnesses. It wasn't dishonesty. It was reluctance, a reluctance to speak.

"I didn't think it was important, I really didn't. And, truth be told, everyone seemed to expect the boy to return sooner or later." His face grew mournful. "But he hasn't."

The man seemed to be telling the truth. There was something else, though, something that was bubbling just below the surface. David couldn't put his finger on it. "So, what is it?" he asked, keeping his posture open, his voice kind. "What is it that you want to tell me?"

The old man swallowed. "I saw something on the field that night. The night the boy disappeared."

It struck David—it was fear. The old man was frightened as hell.

—ᗯᗯ—

Mr Lim tried to focus on the stack of papers he was marking, but it was no good. Despite all that he'd said, he couldn't deny that the whole disappearance had shaken him. Against his will, his mind returned to the footage he and the other teachers had studied so closely for clues months ago.

It'd been spliced together from a few different cameras. Freddie was seen leaving the library by himself. He then reappeared on one of the cameras located at the corridor leading to the canteen. It was clear the boy was heading towards the side gate.

So far, so good.

Then the canteen CCTVs showed him entering. The lights there remained switched on till about 10 p.m. every night, so though the video was a bit fuzzy, there was no doubt it was Freddie. His form teacher, his parents—they were all sure it was him.

From the canteen, he had to cross the field in order to reach the side gate. By then it was around 7.40 p.m., already dark. There were no lights illuminating the field. The only lights were the flood lights, and they were almost never switched on unless there was a match being played on the field. Under ordinary circumstances, the walk through the field from canteen to side gate took no more than two minutes or so—in utter darkness, of course, save for the little oasis of light in the distance coming from the side gate. Mr Lim himself had taken the walk at night many times, and disconcerting as it might be, one could take comfort in the fact that many a teacher and student had come this way for years and years, always without incident. Until now.

Freddie exited the canteen and stepped on to the field at 7.43 p.m., according to the footage. He never reached the side gate. Both Old Wong and the camera above the gate told the same tale: no sign of Freddie at all, not from the time Old Wong took watch to the time the police came. The boy stepped on to the field and was never seen leaving it again.

The police later examined the chain-link fence running along the length of the field, the one that extended from the side gate all the way to the end of the field, where it took a 90-degree turn leftwards and continued, past the breadth of the field, till it was obscured by the classroom block sitting next to the canteen. Mr Lim and some other teachers accompanied the officers. They looked for holes but found none. They scoured the barbed wire crowning the fence for signs of torn clothing, or any material that could have served as protective padding for someone looking to scale the fence. Nothing. In any case, Mr Lim couldn't think of any reason why Freddie would want to leave that way when he could simply walk through the side gate. Even if he intended to run away from home after that.

As the investigation eventually deepened, the entire perimeter of the school premises was checked and rechecked, every gate, every length of fence or wall or whatever it was that separated the school from the outside.

Nothing.

The police had no explanation. No one had any explanation. The official theory was that Freddie had decided to run away from home (never mind why—no one could even figure out *how*), and that had enraged Mr Lim. He knew that if Freddie had been an Express-stream student instead of a Normal Tech one, everyone would have had a more difficult time believing that he had left home without any explanation. But as it stood, no one had any doubts that the boy *must* have been a troubled youth, even if he didn't have any record of delinquency. Academic performance, it seemed, was an accurate indicator of character as well.

Life went on, but every so often, usually just as he thought he'd finally moved on, a familiar black and white image would resurface, unbidden, in his mind: the lone figure of Freddie, stepping away from the light of the canteen and into the silent maw of the inky blackness beyond. For a moment he seemed to hesitate, pivoting on one foot, half-turned towards the safety of the canteen. And every time Mr Lim would silently plead for the boy to turn back, despite having watched the clip umpteen times. And every time Freddie would, after that flicker of hesitation, step into the darkness. In a moment he was gone, swallowed by the void.

Mr Lim glanced at his watch. It was nearly time.

——◦◦◦——

The old man was starting to twitch slightly, as if his seat was heating up in the most uncomfortable way. He asked for a cup of water, and the detective obliged. Two long swallows were enough to empty the paper cup, which then teetered nervously on the table under the thick, vigorous gusts from the air conditioner.

"Lights, sir."

"What do you mean, lights?"

"That's what I saw on the field. The night that boy disappeared."

A knot of unease was growing in David's stomach. When he next spoke he found his voice shot through with an urgency that surprised even himself.

"Tell me *everything*."

——◦◦◦——

The sun was starting to set. In the dying light, the field was ablaze, golden and green. Mr Lim's eyes roved back and forth over the expanse, watchful for any potential dangers, but the verdant plain gazed back with all the innocence of Eden.

The grass was extraordinarily lush, he suddenly realised. In all his years of teaching, all his time at other schools, he had never seen a field free from the bald patches and brittle-brown grass that seemed to plague every school field. Except here. For some reason, that thought made him uncomfortable.

—◦◦◦—

Andy could feel his heart pumping wildly as his eyes flung themselves here and there against an impenetrable cloak of black, straining to see if anyone was creeping up on him.

Tim was right, he thought reluctantly. *This is way more fun than the previous war games.*

Even with every player wearing a light stick, it was close to impossible to make out how near or far a person was. The light stick swung and jumped along with the motion of its wearer, more often than not simply a blur of blue or red. More than once he had thought the enemy to be at least a good 20 metres away or so, only to have a ghostly hand grasp at him the moment he had his back turned. He had screamed in fright no fewer than three times.

He was having the time of his life.

—⁓—

Up on the second-storey podium overlooking the field, Mr Lim was bored. All he could see were dozens of blue and red dots circling each other, sometimes darting forward, sometimes beating a hasty retreat. The cries and laughter floating up from below suggested that the boys were having a much more exciting time than he was. Mr Tay—

"Go get them, boys. Go, go, go!" He was jumping up and down so hard that Mr Lim could feel the podium floor shake slightly every time he landed. The senior teacher grinned in the dark, wishing he shared the other's enthusiasm.

As the battle wore on, fewer and fewer lights remained on the field. Those "killed" gathered on the sidelines, cheering their teammates on. Mr Lim felt his mind starting to wander, only to be brought back brusquely by a gust of the chilly night air.

He froze. A sudden uneasiness had settled upon him, but he couldn't tell why. He turned to Mr Tay, who was almost a silhouette, even though he was right beside him. He was stiffly silent.

"What's wrong?" Mr Lim heard himself whispering.

"L-look."

He couldn't see where Mr Tay was pointing at in the dark, so he ran his eyes over the field again and again.

He saw it—a *green* light. No, green lights. They were floating about at the periphery, far from the thick of the action, about the same size as each of the handful of blue and red light sticks remaining. A sudden frisson of fear coursed through him, but he forced himself to be rational.

"Probably just the referees or something. Umpire. Whatever you call it."

"Probably." Mr Tay's voice rang out hollowly. "Yes, yes, you must be right."

But Mr Lim knew he hadn't seen the green lights earlier in the night, only now. Or was that really the case? There was that video on YouTube, he recalled, the one with the gorilla amongst the basketball players. You were told to count the number of passes or something, and you just never noticed the gorilla as it ambled among the players. *You don't see the things you don't expect to be there*, he thought. The boys had forgotten to mention there would be referees wearing green lights, that's all. He was letting his imagination run wild, the precise thing he'd told Mr Tay not to do.

"The lights, did they move?"

The old man nodded.

David felt his blood run cold. "So the lights were being carried by someone." His voice grew angry.

"You should have told us this earlier. That could have been the boy's abductors."

Mr Wong shook his head vigorously. "It couldn't be. They moved too fast. And they could change direction in a split second." His gnarled finger zig-zagged the air, tracing an erratic path.

David leaned back, arms crossed. It was all too absurd, the stuff of urban legends, not something you'd want to hear in a witness testimony. "What else? This time, leave *nothing* unsaid." He made sure to allow an ominous undertone to creep into his voice.

"There…there is a particular moment I remember. It seemed so…unnatural, I couldn't shake it from my mind for a long time after that."

David waited.

The old man continued: "There was a moment when the lights all suddenly darted forward, then stopped."

"So?"

"Have you seen people throwing chicken carcasses to crocodiles before? I have, when I was a child. It's the same type of movement. One moment they are all still, and the next, all you can see is a vicious blur, muscles and jaws. And then it stops, just like that. Like nothing ever happened. But if you look closely, you can see what remains…"

The inspector's eyes narrowed.

The old man's final words were almost a whisper. "The lights, they moved just like that. It was as if they found what they were looking for."

—⁓—

Andy was exhausted. He was the last of the reds, and there were still two blues he had to contend with. He didn't think he would have the strength to defeat them both. They were playing it smart. They kept themselves far apart, so he had to constantly swivel his head left and right to make sure one of them hadn't snuck up on him while he was focused on the other. His head was starting to feel heavy, and his thighs throbbed. Oddly enough, he felt cold. The droplets of sweat clinging to his skin felt like frost.

I'm even starting to imagine things, he thought. He had caught sight of flashes of green a few times now, only to see nothing when he looked again more carefully. Only the screaming trickling in from the edge of the field kept him going, but they sounded so soft and seemed so far away.

The sound of something snapping yanked his attention back. It came from some distance away, invisible in the darkness, and it sounded as if someone had stepped on a twig.

Shit! With a start, he realised he had lost sight of one of the blues, and he had only looked away for a second. The other one was still there, to his left, pacing, waiting for the right time to strike, but— he spun around wildly to his right, half-expecting a suddenly close-up blue light to be screaming in his face, but only a solid sheet of black met him. The night wind curled its icy fingers around his arms and legs, and he could feel the goosebumps rising.

"Just what sort of stupid trick is this!" he yelled at the remaining blue light. He felt a bit better, now that the still silence was broken. "You're not supposed to hide your light stick, you cheaters!"

The blue light came to a standstill. "I don't know where he went either, man." It was Tim's voice. "Is that you, Andy?"

"Yeah. Who's that with you?"

"You mean the other blue? I have no—"

"No," Andy cut in, his blood curdling. "The green—"

—⁓—

As the scream rose shrilly into the night, Mr Lim was already racing down the stairs.

Just moments ago, he and Mr Tay had watched in disbelief as one of the green lights lunged towards one of the blues with unearthly speed and, in the blink of an eye, both lights went out. As suddenly as if a thick dark cloth had been thrown over them.

Then, another green light started creeping up towards the remaining blue.

"Go to the control room, now!" he had shouted at Mr Tay. He could feel his hair standing on end. "Turn the damn flood lights on."

Now, tearing down the stairs two steps at a time, he could feel a feral fear gripping his insides. *Please, please let it be just some stupid prank.*

The boys on the edge of the field were eerily silent, their red and blue lights dead-still. *Not spinning like the red and blue police lights that fateful night*, he thought distantly. In the growing glow of the flood lights, Mr Lim could just make out their pale, frightened faces. "What happened!" he almost screamed, as he tore past them and on to the field.

His skin recoiled at the unnatural chill that suddenly enveloped him.

The flood lights behind him were getting brighter, like some sort of alien dawn breaking on a strange planet. He could make out a lone figure out in the open, unmoving. It made no noise, said nothing. Didn't even turn as his thundering footsteps approached. Supercharged with adrenaline, he did not slow down. If it was anyone—*anything*—but one of his students, it would bear the brunt of his wrath.

"Andy! Andy!" Recognising the boy, the teacher grabbed his student's shoulders and spun him around. The boy screamed and clawed at him like a wild animal until, as if overcome by exhaustion—or fear—he collapsed in his arms.

The lights were at full power now, and it was as bright as noon. From where he stood he could see the entire extent of the field.

Empty.

He heard something crunch under his feet. A light stick, brutally snapped in two, the blue fluid in it spilling from the jagged edges, already pooling like blood at his feet.

PENANCE

The first time Mr Lee came to see me, I knew, about ten minutes in, that he was different from the rest. He was the very picture of a successful young executive—he was a lawyer, as it turned out—a fashionable haircut, finely tailored clothes and most of all, that tell-tale swagger of a man accustomed to having his way.

That image held, until he opened his mouth. He spoke quickly, too quickly—impossibly quickly.

"You've got to slow down a little, Mr Lee," I said. I'd seen patients like that. A mind with too much on it for the mouth to do it justice, no matter how fast it moved. Like a vast reservoir being forced through a tiny spigot. Imagine the unbearable pressure, the immense strain on the sole, inadequate outlet. Mr Lee was all that and more. More than I'd ever seen in anyone who'd passed through my clinic in decades of practice.

"I'm sorry—I'll try." His reply was immediate, reflexive. Like he'd been told that countless times before. The tempo of his speech slowed enough to be intelligible. "I know I have this problem. And it's getting out of hand."

"So that's why you're here to see me?"

He nodded, the strain of speaking more slowly more than apparent on his face. His eyes and the corners of his mouth twitched as if they had a life of their own, quickened by a manic pulse of electricity that coursed through his features every few seconds or so. It was exhausting enough to watch, and I could only imagine what it had to be like for him.

"It's driving me crazy," he whispered.

I uttered some sympathetic words, and I found myself meaning them. Forgive me for sounding callous, but after so long it's sometimes difficult to feel sympathy as acutely as when I first started out. It becomes an act of will rather than an impulse of the heart. But something about this man made it impossible to fall back on the shopworn platitudes I was used to bandying about.

"Does it pose a problem at work?" I asked.

"It did at first. Some clients complained. But eventually I was able to rein it in, so no, I don't think it's really an issue at work. Inside though"—he tapped his temple—"inside I can feel my mind burning up."

"How long have you had this issue?"

I looked up from my note-taking. It was the first time he hadn't responded immediately.

"Ever since—ever since the accident."

"Ah. A car accident?"

"Yes. But it didn't involve me." He licked his lips. He clearly had more to say, only he didn't know if he should. "At least, not really."

I put down my pen. "Perhaps you should start from the beginning." I gave him my most reassuring smile. He didn't respond.

"I'm not sure it's really relevant, to be honest," he said finally.

"Mr Lee, if we are to go to the root of the problem," I said gently, "it is important that you loop me in."

"Doctor," he said, "could you just, I don't know, prescribe something that would relax me? A sedative or something, perhaps."

I did as he asked, and he left.

He was back two days later. He burst into the consultation room with a suddenness more befitting an excitable child, and he strode right up to me and seized my hand.

"Please," he said, speaking even more quickly than before, "please, you have to help me, Doctor. I'm going crazy." At least, I think that's what he said. It wasn't the words that conveyed the message, but the crazed look in his eyes.

I did a quick physical examination, pulse, blood pressure, all that. Nothing was wrong with him.

"I think, Mr Lee, that you really need to tell me about what happened. I can't help you otherwise." There was, I have to admit, a certain curiosity bubbling up within me. How might a car accident have caused this? Head trauma? But wait—he had said he hadn't been involved. Curiouser and curiouser.

A look of despair came over his face. The spasmodic twitching of his eyes and mouth I noticed in the previous session were still evident, and it seemed, if anything, that they had worsened.

"Now, you mentioned a car accident previously. How long ago was that?"

He rambled something.

"You really have to speak more slowly, Mr Lee."

"Aboutamonthago." With a little effort, I finally could make out what he was saying.

"So what happened?"

"I was driving to work. There was this car in front of me all the way, from the time I turned out from my place. A Toyota. We were on the right-most lane but he was going impossibly slowly. Below the speed limit, even. I was furious. There I was, almost late for work, and there he was dawdling along. I high-beamed him, honked at him, but it was no use. Traffic was fairly heavy, so I couldn't overtake from the left lane either.

"I saw it. I didn't see it straight away, but I saw it eventually. The P-plate, that orange triangle. He was a new driver. That only made me angrier. An inexperienced driver who insisted on driving like a snail had no business driving on the right-most lane. Then he signalled, and it was clear why he'd been hogging the right lane. He was making a right turn, the very same turn I was going to take. I cursed and swore. There was nothing worse than waiting in line behind a new driver who had shown himself to be afraid of exceeding the speed limit by even the slightest. I turned out to be right. He missed every opportunity to take the turn, even when the only oncoming vehicle, a trailer, was way off in the distance. I lost it then. I blared the horn, held it down. He inched forward, jumpy, afraid—I should have stopped then. I should have, but I didn't.

"Then, at the worst possible moment, just as the oncoming trailer was coming dangerously close, and with my horn still blaring, the poor guy decided to take the turn. I think he took the trailer driver by surprise too, for he took a second or two to react, to brake, and by then it was too late. The trailer had too much momentum, and it ploughed—my god, it just ploughed into the Toyota like it was an aluminium can."

He was pale now, and breaking out in a bit of a sweat. I offered him a bottle of water, which he accepted with a hurried thank you. He wrenched off the cap and took a few swallows before continuing.

"It was horrible, horrible. The terrible crunching sound, the scream of the splintering glass. I ran out from my vehicle to see if I could help, but even from a distance I knew it was going to be futile. The car was a mangled wreck. Can you imagine what I was going through? It was my fault—mine—even if in the eyes of the law I wasn't guilty. And the driver, the poor guy—my god, I could see him through the twisted metal, see his blood-streaked face, his lifeless eyes staring right back at me. He looked young. Terribly young."

With trembling fingers he reached for the bottle. I made a show of jotting down a sentence or two, though I had no idea what I was writing. The only sound breaking through the silence of my consultation room was his heavy breathing.

"We can take a break, if you like," I offered.

"No, no. I'm nearly finished." He took yet another swig at the bottle. "So, yes. His eyes, staring back at me. It was unnerving. It was terrifying. It's like he knew, you see. Even in death he knew I was the one responsible, the one who had pushed him to take the turn he hadn't wanted to. I didn't dare to go too close. The trailer driver was already by his side— as close he could get, anyway, reaching into the carnage, feeling for a pulse. He looked at me and shook his head. There was this terrible stricken look on the trailer driver's face. He was a foreign worker, a

Bangladeshi, it looked like, and it was clear he knew he was in hot soup. I thought he was going to yell at me, blame me for causing the accident, but he did nothing of that sort. There was just this pleading look on his face—it was like he was saying to me, over and over again, 'This isn't my fault, right? This can't be my fault.'

"As it turned out, the police did think it was his fault. They charged him with negligent driving, though I'm not sure if has gone to trial. When the police took my statement I told them everything... everything but the part where I hounded the guy to take the turn. I just *couldn't*, you know?"

He stopped. I waited, and when he didn't resume talking, I spoke.

"So was that when the problems started?"

He nodded. "When it first started, I thought there was something wrong with my body. My mind, it seemed, was perfectly fine. It was my body that couldn't keep up. When I spoke my mouth felt like rubber, thick and slow, and the words I wanted to say just couldn't get through quickly enough. It's like, you're at the helm of a ship, a massive ship, and for every action you take you set the course and the speed, then you sit back and wait for the floating behemoth to respond, for it to swing round and act on your directive—and all this time, what the hell do you do? You wait! By god, you wait! That's what it's like in my head, sitting around waiting for my thoughts and wants to be realised. Do you know how much time there is? I could command and countermand and counter-countermand and my hand wouldn't even have started moving yet. And you know what comes to mind while waiting, what pops up every time? I see his face. His eyes. I see those bloody, lifeless orbs staring vacantly at me, and I know his vengeance is upon me.

"And you know what's the worst part? It's speeding up. It's going faster and faster and faster. Soon I'll be spending an eternity in my mind—nothing but me and my thoughts, and *him*. And not a single person around me will realise what's going on. I'd be a prisoner in my own body."

He was looking at me now. For a moment I thought the twitching in his eyes had gone away— and then I realised: it was so fast now it was almost a blur. You could hardly see the eyelids moving. But what frightened me most was his gaze. It was like staring into an empty window. Every now and then I thought I saw a flicker of life, an awful awareness of the plight he was in. But mostly it was glazed over, as if the mind had gone some place else. For his sake I hoped that was so.

"He doesn't speak." His words caught me off-guard. "God, it would be a mercy if he at least said anything or even laughed at my misery! But no, nothing. He only stares. He only stares. *God.*" His hands shot up to his head, and he began a horrible clawing motion, as if trying to expunge the haunting image from his mind. "*Help me, for fuck's sake, help me!*" It was a warped, raspy sound, and I would have had difficulty making them out if not for the outstretched, flailing hands making their meaning clear. They were thrashing like eels out of water, uncontrollably. Violently.

He was screaming now. A grating, full-blown screech that scraped my nerves raw. "Helpmehelpmehelpmehelpmehelpme!" His arms surged forward blindly, grasping, clawing. I stumbled back in alarm.

What could I do? I could only think of one thing. Grabbing a syringe, I drew out some diazepam and seized his arm. It took more than three tries—he was strong, and his arm was flashing about so frenetically that it felt like I was trying to grab a hissing cobra. When I finally caught it I had to pin it down with my knee as I administered the injection. I could swear I heard a wheeze of relief as the sedative took, and I had to lunge forward to grab his crumpling body as he deflated like a balloon.

"Everything okay, Doctor?" It was Susan, my nurse-cum-receptionist, speaking through the small window through which I passed her prescriptions and the like. Panting slightly, I squatted, my hand still on the patient—just in case—so I could look through the opening at eye level. Her concerned eyes stared back at me.

"Call IMH, Susan. I think we need their help."

———~~~———

"What happened?" The utter quiet of the sterile white corridor unsettled me. I strode rapidly, feeling a slight tingling in my fingers. It was freezing. The orderly accompanying me looked very stiff in his crisp white uniform. He wouldn't look me in the eye.

"I think you should see for yourself, Doctor."

"You were supposed to take proper care of him, dammit."

"Believe me, sir, we tried our best. We really did." He stopped. "The past two months have been… difficult, to say the least."

Through the endless labyrinth we wound, deeper and deeper towards the dreadful core. Heads turned as we passed by, or so I thought. Voices dropped to a whisper.

"Didn't you keep him sedated?"

"We did, sir. For the most part. But you can't keep a patient on sedatives 24/7. We had to get him off them for a while. That's when *it* happened."

"*What* happened?" I was getting annoyed by the evasion, but he stared ahead resolutely, unseeingly.

"We're nearly there, sir."

We were at the padded cells. For patients who tried to hurt themselves. I noticed, for the first time, that the orderly's uniform wasn't as spotless as I had thought. A small scarlet smudge adorned his sleeve. It looked like blood. I pointed it out to him.

"Must have been a patient," he offered. Then he turned away and said nothing more, at least not until we reached the door of Isolation Unit 6.

"Here we are. Would you like me to accompany you inside?" He was already edging away from the door, as if expecting—or hoping—I wouldn't take up his offer.

"He is sedated now, isn't he?"

"He is, sir."

"Very well. I think I should be fine on my own."

The door swung open silently. I braced myself.

He was standing in a corner. Absolutely still, his back towards me. The upper dome of his head was wrapped in bandages. I took a slow step inside.

I jumped as the door slammed shut behind me.

I stared. The little speech I had prepared mentally was gone, jettisoned from my mind. I simply stared.

He finally moved, slowly. His hands crept towards the thick gauze and touched it gingerly, as if assessing the damage. Fingertips roved across the white expanse—well, mostly white. There were spots where the blood had seeped through, and he seemed to know this, for his fingers would linger over these spots. Caressing, almost.

"HelloDoctor."

I flinched. In the deathly silence of the chamber, his voice seemed gut-wrenchingly loud. It stabbed at me, not my ears, but my stomach. I felt sick.

"H-how are you, Mr Lee?"

"Greatgreat.Neverbeenbetter.Neverbeenbetter."

I still couldn't see his face, but I could hear the grin in his voice. I steeled myself and forced a step forward. Then another. My hand reached out to touch his shoulder—

"Wha-what are you doing?" I sputtered.

His fingers were now twitching manically, like blind, spitting snakes. They crawled, spasmodically, all over the base of his skull, burrowing futilely against the coarse cloth.

They stopped. Clenched between his thumb and finger was a slip of white. The loose end of the bandage.

"Mr Lee!" I stood, frozen, as he began to unwrap the bandage. His movements were now slow, methodical. I thought he was taking extra care in removing the gauze, but it soon dawned on me what it was. It was a performance. No, an unveiling.

I thought about calling for the orderly, but even with his back to me the patient seemed to divine my intentions, for he raised a calm hand. His other hand continued its steady circular motion, and the length of white that trailed from it grew redder and wetter as it grew longer. Finally, he stopped. Much of the red and white python lay coiled at his feet, with only just the tail end snaking up his body. I watched, hypnotised, as he pulled at the last bit that was still stuck somewhere on his forehead, and it came away with a sickening tearing sound.

"I—want—to—show—you—something." He was speaking slowly now. It was clear he wanted to be understood.

I could taste my lunch at the back of my throat. "Please, Mr Lee, please." I didn't know what I was pleading for. "Please…"

"He wouldn't go away, you see. He wouldn't go away. Everywhere I turned, I saw him. The boy, the poor, poor boy…"

He was turning now.

"I had to make him go away, you understand?"

As I looked upon his monstrous visage, a scream wrenched its way out of my body. My knees buckled, and before I knew it I was on the ground.

He loomed over me, his fingers at where his eyes once were. They gently traced the rims of the two gaping voids, and below them his mouth broke into a grotesque grin.

"You know what the funny thing is? I can still see him now. Funny, isn't it?"

The door swung open with a loud crash, and I felt myself being carried out of the dreadful room.

"Please, sir, you have to stop screaming." A disembodied voice rang out from somewhere above me. *"Sir, please—Eric, hand me the syringe."*

The darkness around me grew warm and fuzzy, pulling me towards it. But *he* remained, staring, his empty sockets drilling into me.

And he began to laugh.

FINDING DAWN

She knew she ought to have left hours ago, but the desolate beauty of the wetlands had kept her lingering there, long after night had fallen and shrouded all there was to see. If she squinted, she thought, she could almost still see the pale wind turbines dotting the headland, forlornly watching the sea. But in truth she could see nothing. The night had fallen too deep.

A chilly wind rose with a soft keening, drawing with it the hair on her skin, till they stood on end. The taxi driver had been right. Out here alone, she was vulnerable, not just physically, but emotionally, spiritually. What was it the driver had said? *Purge all sad thoughts from your mind, miss. Nothing attracts them like negative emotions.*

Them? she had asked. *What's them?*

He gave her a meaningful glance. Once, he said, he had come out to the Gaomei Wetlands after a fight with his mother. To let off steam, and also to fish. Dusk arrived, and still he stayed. No way he was going to go home to get himself another earful. His heart still simmering, he baited the hook and cast his rod. Only when the last light had died out, making it impossible to see, did he begin to fumble about blindly to gather his things.

His hand found something cold.

Fingers, moving.

Don't stay past dusk, he warned again.

Too late for her. She couldn't move anywhere, not in such utter darkness. Or… She could hear the gentle roar of the waves in the distance, so maybe if she stepped *away* from them she could—

She whimpered as her foot sunk into something soft. Mud, or so she hoped. She felt a paralysing fear swell within her. One false move and she could twist her ankle, or worse. No, she had to stay put for the entire night, rooted to one spot, and hope for the best. Hope that nothing in the night would find her, cowering and shackled by her inability to see even her own outstretched hand.

She lowered herself slowly, patting the ground gingerly to make sure it was clear. It was, but her hands returned damp. Reluctantly, her fingers crawled further afield, ready to shrink back at the slightest touch of something alien, but all they found was more wetness. With a defeated sigh, she sat down. The cold slowly trickled in.

Purge all sad thoughts, didn't the taxi driver say? Heh, where to begin? Adrift in the world, without anchor, with no sense of up and down or east and west. The one fixed point in her life, her one mooring, was lost forever. Can one possibly banish a thought, a feeling like that?

Warmth brimmed in her eyes and rolled down her cheeks.

That's when she heard it. Breathing. It seemed so close that she couldn't believe she hadn't heard it before. She held her breath and listened with a panicked desperation. It was unmistakable—the slow intake of air, followed by a sigh-like release. She felt her body freeze up, a primal pause as it considered whether to fight or flee.

"Hey, hey, it's okay. Relax." It was a man's voice. She felt the skin on her face tighten uncomfortably as her body involuntarily drew everything inward to protect itself. "It's okay, really." The pounding in her chest and ears crescendoed—until a question rose above the hubbub and demanded to be answered. Why was he, or it, speaking English? Out here in the far-flung outskirts of Taichung, Taiwan, surely everyone, even the ghosts, spoke Mandarin.

Something in her mind clicked. He was a tourist, like her. Human, flesh and blood. And like her, he hadn't left when everyone else had, after seeing the sun melt into the sea.

"W-who are you?" she squeaked. "Are you a tourist?"

"Yes, I suppose so."

"You're not sure?"

He gave a soft, sheepish laugh. "No, I am. It's just that I've been here so many times that I don't know whether I should call myself a tourist anymore."

She felt her heart beating a little slower. "You're Singaporean, aren't you?" she said, feeling the familiar accent bring an oddly comforting rush of warmth. "You came out here to watch the sunset?"

"Yep. It was beautiful, huh?"

"Yeah. It's…it's so peaceful here." She took a deep breath, savouring the fresh, slightly salty air. "Helps you to forget your troubles."

There was a slight hesitation before the voice spoke. "You, you have troubles?"

"Don't we all?"

An agreeable silence. The waves roared as they swept in, sighed as they pulled back. From far away a seabird called, perhaps seeking out its mate. It called again and again, its cry echoing in the void, and nothing answered.

The voice spoke. "So, what's troubling you?"

After a period of silence, and perhaps sensing her reluctance to speak, it continued: "I'll start with mine, then. I lost my fiancée, years and years ago. Every year I come here to remember, to grieve."

Something in his voice touched her. "She died?"

"Cancer."

"I'm sorry," she murmured. "You never moved on?"

"I tried. After some years, I started dating again. But...I just *couldn't*, you know? I saw her face in every girl I met. Heard her voice, her laugh."

She sighed. "Sometimes they never really leave, do they?"

She heard nothing, but could have sworn he nodded. She felt it.

"It's like there's always this little part of her with me," the voice said at last. "And it makes everything hurt like hell. The slightest thing can remind me of her again, and it hurts like she just died yesterday. But the funny thing is, even if I could, I wouldn't want that feeling to go away. It's all I have left of her. I know it doesn't really make any sense."

"No, no. I think I know what you mean."

The silence grew, expectant. Did she—did she really want to bare it all? It didn't seem...appropriate. He was a stranger, and one she couldn't even see at that. But *that* was it—something about the darkness was strangely liberating. She could tell him anything, everything, and she would never have to look him in the eye after that. She wouldn't even know it if she passed him on the street. A voice in the dark, that's all he was.

"You know what I was doing while it was still bright? I walked to the end of the boardwalk. It was high tide." There, she had stood at world's end.

There, the endless sea had spread itself before her, beckoning. She had sat down, dipping her toes in, then her feet, ankles, knees. The sea was loving, warm. "I sat there, and I thought of nothing but him. Him and us."

"What happened?"

The words just tumbled out. "Four years, you know? Four perfect years. Our flat was coming. He proposed only last month."

Perhaps a part of her always knew it was too good to be true, too good to last.

"Then out of the blue, he broke off the engagement," she said. "Said it wasn't what he wanted. Said he felt trapped in the relationship."

"I'm sorry to hear that."

"I just couldn't wrap my head around it, you know? We did everything right. But now it's like everything had been a pretence, a lie. That it was only me loving him all this time."

"I'm sure that's not true."

"Then *how*?" she found herself shouting. "How do you go from loving someone to just, to just—*nothing*." She buried her face in her knees, feeling her breaths grow ragged. "He was all I had…"

The thickening silence pressed onto her ears.

"I'm sorry," she said at last. "I don't even know you, and here I am…"

"No, it's okay."

The seabird was still calling, and the waves continued to crash and retreat. Life went on. And that, really, had to be the hardest part. Knowing that his world went on without her, while hers had ground to a standstill.

"Sometimes," she said fiercely, "I think it's better to lose a loved one to death, than to have them leave you like that, to want nothing to do with you." Her words were flung out wildly, blindly, from a place of hurt she hadn't even known existed. They ought to have shocked her, but they didn't. "Tell me honestly," she continued, feeling her face grow hot, "tell me you'd rather she be alive but with someone else."

"Well...I must admit, that's really difficult to answer."

"*Exactly.*"

As her sudden fury subsided, her face remained hot, but now with shame. "I'm sorry, that was insensitive of me. And selfish. I ought to be happy that he's happy doing whatever it is that makes him happy, even if it's not with me."

"Well," he said, his voice somewhat wistful, "we're only human."

Eager to change the subject, she asked, "Why do you come all the way here to remember her?"

"It's a special place for the both of us. And..."

She waited.

"And it was here that I first spoke to her. *After* she died."

A chill thrilled through her body. "You can talk to spirits?"

"Yes. Apparently I've had the ability since I was a boy, or so my mother tells me. But I've never done it much. Until my fiancée died."

"Why's her spirit here? Was this where she…"

"Oh, no. From what I've experienced, spirits linger in places that are important to them. It could be where they died, or anywhere else. For Vivian, this place is where we shared a lot of our happy memories together."

"Is she here right now?" she asked, feeling the spasm of a shiver twist her stomach.

"No, no." He gave a small laugh. "Oh, she wouldn't hurt you anyway. But she's moved on. To a better place, I'm sure."

"And yet you still come here?"

"Well, this is a happy place for us. Besides, ever since she's left I've…never mind."

She waited for him to change his mind, to speak, but he stayed resolutely silent.

"This place has a special place in my heart too," she said. "It's where he proposed to me. I suppose it's silly, but I came here hoping to, I don't know, maybe relive some of the memories?"

"That makes sense."

A question struck her. "Why did—Vivian, was it?—how…why did she move on?"

"I told her to." There was a catch in his voice. "I told her it was time to let go, to let me go."

For a moment, she considered the revelation in silence. "I don't know if I could do it if I were you."

"It wasn't easy. I wanted her around. But I couldn't be selfish. She wasn't going to have any peace until she left." His voice was full, almost overflowing. "Sometimes if you love someone, you just have to let them go."

They sat there in the darkness, hearing nothing but the waves from afar. Like the sighs of a pensive giant, inexorable, unending. There was no knowing how long they stayed there, not speaking, just listening to the passage of time.

"I wish I could sit here forever," she said suddenly. Here, where time stood still, where she didn't have to deal with losing him. Her mind could remain a complete blank, and her eyes could stare unseeingly into the lovely loneliness that lay all around her, for all time.

"You have to move on eventually. There are still good things out there, waiting, you know?" There was a significant edge in his voice, and she was sure that if she could see him, his eyes would be fixed on her, trying to tell her something his words couldn't— or wouldn't.

"No...I have nothing..." She could feel the life seeping out of her, something within her disintegrating, leaking, carried away by the wind. That's what she wanted—to break off into tiny pieces, to be dispersed and scattered like sand in the breeze...

"Grace," the voice was now sharp, urgent, pulling her back. "Grace, listen to me. Do you remember how you got here? Do you remember anything at all?"

"How do you know my name?" she asked weakly. More time than she reckoned had to have passed; there cracked a grey line in the distance, fast widening, heralding the coming of a new day.

"Grace, you walked to the end of the boardwalk, remember? What happened then?"

She had dipped her toes in, hadn't she? Yes, the water was so warm. So welcoming.

"What happened next? What did you do?"

Nothing, she'd done nothing else... The water, it'd reached her ankles, then her knees.

A growing horror ballooned in her stomach. *No... No!*

The water was at her stomach now, then her shoulders, her head. She let herself drift into the waiting murkiness.

"I...I drowned." The words sounded foreign in her mouth, and yet her voice betrayed no surprise.

Somehow, she'd known all this time; a secret her mind had tucked into a deep recess, hoping to forget.

"Yes, Grace. You killed yourself. You remember now." She thought she heard relief in his voice.

"Who are you? Why are you doing this?" Her body felt weak. The horizon was brimming with light, and it hurt her eyes.

"I'm who I said I was. Everything I told you was true. It's time to move on, Grace. Move into the light, the dawn."

"I, I can't," she sobbed. "I can't leave him. Kai Shiong...Kai Shiong..."

"You have to let him go, Grace. Remember what I said? Sometimes if you love someone, you have to let them go."

"Kai Shiong..." Her voice was fading, almost gone. The glare filled her vision, burning everything out. The last thing she saw was the white wind turbines gleaming in the sun. They no longer looked like lonesome figures. They looked so brave, staring into the rising sun...

—◦◦◦—

"Thank you, Mr Ong," the young man said. He shook hands with a much older-looking man.

"Just call me Richard."

"She…she's moved on, right?"

The older man sighed. "Yes, I think so."

"Why didn't she see me?" The young man's voice was flat, and his eyes lingered on the now-gleaming expanse of silver that stretched to the horizon.

"She was engulfed in her grief, Kai Shiong. I only managed to reach her because of my ability."

"I—" He choked, and hurriedly swallowed several times before speaking again. "I would have liked to say goodbye, I guess. Say sorry." His eyes shone, and his voice shook: "And to tell her I love her."

The older man was silent for a moment. "We don't always get a chance to," he finally said. There was no reproach in his voice. "Be happy with the time you had with her."

"You're not going to ask me why I left her?"

"It's not important anymore." He paused and, while pretending to shade his eyes from the sun, studied the younger man for a moment. A look of pity swept into his shadowed eyes. "Come," he said, placing a hand on the young man's shoulder, "it's time to go."

And the two men walked away from the sun.

THE UNSEEN OCCUPANT

In 2010, the Singapore government, worried about escalating house prices, introduced the Seller's Stamp Duty in a bid to discourage the flipping of property in a rapidly heating market. The very next year, my friend Terence sold his newly purchased HDB flat barely a month after the completion of the transaction, thereby being the only person I know to incur a hefty 16 per cent stamp duty on a sale of property. In the circumstances, of course, one can hardly blame him, as I'm sure you'll agree when you've heard the story.

"This isn't America," I said, grinning. "No law to say that the seller has to warn you that the apartment is haunted."

Terence didn't smile. "I couldn't sleep the entire night, and all you can think of doing is to make jokes at my expense."

Chastened, I forced the smile off my lips. It was difficult. Terence had been so pleased with his purchase, from the moment he had signed the Option to Purchase all the way till legal completion two months later. For those two months I had to listen to him go on interminably about the virtues of his incredible find, about how it was a steal at the price the owner was asking, and how he couldn't wait to move into his new place. So I'm sure you'll understand that I couldn't help but savour the irony a little when, after the very first night at his new place, he came to me with his face white as a sheet.

Lo and behold, the flat was haunted.

"Aiyah, friend," I said, putting on my most comforting voice, "not that I want to rub it in or anything, but shouldn't it have struck you as odd that the owner was willing to let it go at such a low price?"

"He had a good reason for it," Terence said sullenly. "His wife had just decided to leave him out of the blue, and he wanted to leave the country to start afresh. Said he was going to Australia or something. Seemed believable at the time."

I shook my head at his credulity. "People will say anything to get rid of haunted property. You should have checked."

"Check? How to check? Call up his relatives and friends to ask if his wife had really left him?"

Good point. I let it slide. "All right, all right, what's done is done. Now tell me what happened, and then we'll see what can be done."

He gave a sigh and a nervous little rub of his palms.

"As you know, I didn't bother with any major renovation. The place was in pretty good shape, considering its age. Been through two owners before me." *A-ha!* I wanted to yell. *Betcha the seller didn't say a single word about the previous owner. Guess what happened to him.* He continued: "I just moved in my own furniture—tables, chairs, bed, the lot. Took the whole of yesterday. I was tired as hell, and the bed and mattress were ready—no sheets, but what the hell, I knew I would fall asleep the moment my head hit the pillow."

Terence was a bachelor. Hitting the magical age of 35 had allowed him to finally get a HDB flat of his own, so perhaps I had been unkind to begrudge him his fair share of excitement over his first home. Goodness knows how left behind he must have felt all those years, watching his peers marry and move into their own homes while he languished in his parents' cramped three-room flat.

"I was asleep before I knew it. When I awoke, it was dark, and it being a strange environment and all, I found myself a little scared. So at first I thought it was nothing. Strange new home, strange new sounds to get used to. It was a murmur—no, more like a whistling kind of whisper. Sounded like water going through the pipes."

I nodded understandingly. The things that go bump in the night. Every new home-owner needs at least a month or so to get used to it, and that's with someone you know sleeping beside you. I couldn't imagine what it had to be like to go through all of that alone.

"That's when I started being able to make out some of the words. 'Please' something something. 'Go away' or something like that. I freaked, man, I freaked. I jumped out of bed and ran. Flagged down a taxi at 4 a.m. in nothing but my T-shirt and shorts. Taxi uncle must have thought I was nuts. Luckily I didn't wake my parents up. When they found me sleeping in my room this morning, they just assumed I'd got home late, after they had already slept."

I looked at my friend thoughtfully. I had never known him to be the fanciful sort. He and I were army buddies, and trust me when I say that in the army there are plenty of chances to be scared of what's lying in wait in the dark. Especially when you're out in the forest, trying to ward off the mosquitoes just long enough to be able to fall asleep on the hard, lumpy ground. Terence had slept through everything without a whimper. But still…

"You must have imagined it lah. I mean, it was a new place, and you were stressed from the moving."

"So you think I imagined hearing voices?" He looked at me almost hopefully, as if hearing me tell him how ridiculous he was being would bring him immeasurable comfort.

"Hmm. Maybe there were sounds, and you interpreted them as voices."

He looked relieved. "Must be, must be." He hesitated. "Gary, I know it's weird, but do you think you could just spend one night at my apartment with me? Oh my god," he said, turning slightly red, "that sounded wrong. I mean, just for me to have some peace of mind. You can sleep on the bed. I'll use a sleeping bag."

I made a face. "Really kind of weird, dude. We're a bit too old to have a sleepover."

"Please, man. You know I wouldn't ask unless I'm really worried."

"Fine, fine. Tonight? I'll tell Lin."

After duly informing the wife that I would be spending the night with an old army buddy (and having Terence confirm it in a separate phone call—she's inclined to get suspicious and jealous rather easily, I'm afraid), I found myself at Terence's new apartment, work laptop and iPad in tow, just in case.

"Just like guard duty," I joked. "But now with laptop and iPad."

He grinned weakly.

As it turned out, the evening passed quickly with us reminiscing about the old times, the quirky people we'd known, the beauties and hotties we'd tried in vain to woo and, as people near middle age are wont to do, lamenting how quickly our youth was passing us by. A carton of beers and a few shots of whisky later, I was on the bed, barely conscious, and he was burrowing into his sleeping bag groggily.

When I next opened my eyes there was nothing but blackness. A momentary panic seized me—before my brain eventually remembered where I was. And as my bare wakefulness grew into alertness, a different kind of fear wrenched my gut.

There was a voice. A woman's voice.

My blood ran cold. There was a reason I had found it difficult to believe Terence's story when I first heard it. I didn't believe in ghosts. But in the pitch dark, my hearing agonisingly acute, there was no doubt about what I was hearing. I couldn't make out the words, but the murmuring was definitely in a female voice.

I drove my toe into the cocoon that held Terence. Hard. He awoke with a small cry.

"Wha—"

"Shhh," I ordered. "Listen."

A momentary rustling of the sleeping bag, then silence. When he finally spoke he sounded like a little boy. "Y-you hear that too?"

I didn't bother to answer. Now that he was awake and I was no longer alone, I was emboldened. I crept out of bed and felt for the light switch.

The voice persisted in the light-bleached room.

"It's coming from outside," I said, grabbing my friend by the shoulder. "Quick, let's go."

"What the hell are you doing?" he whispered fiercely, his eyes wide.

"We have to find out where it's coming from."

He shook his head wildly. "No fucking way. Are you freaking crazy?"

"Look, there's either a natural explanation for this, or there isn't. We have to find out which." I didn't say more, but deep in my heart I desperately wanted it to be the former. A recording of some sort playing, I thought, or perhaps even music from an inconsiderate neighbour.

Terence followed me reluctantly out of the room. The voice was louder, clearer, but the words still unintelligible. I switched on every light I could find. Hearing the voice in a hallway steeped in light didn't exactly make it any less eerie. If anything, it added to the surreality of it all. There was a certain edge to the voice—sorrow, perhaps, or something more malicious. It was starting to sound less and less like music.

"Shit, shit. I can't do this, man." Terence was nearly whimpering now. "Listen to it, for goodness sake.

It can't be anything natural. Or good." He leaned against the wall, his cheek and palms flat against it, as if he were clinging to it for dear life.

I grunted in disgust. To be honest, I think what kept me going was the rock-solid certainty I had within me that there was a natural explanation to it all. I didn't—*couldn't*—for even a moment countenance any other explanation.

"Please…" the soft voice moaned, echoing slightly in the stillness. It appeared that Terence was right about that word at least. I looked at him, still heaped against the wall. He was quivering like a mass of gelatine. He was going to be of no use.

I followed the sound into the living room and turned on the lights. Here, it seemed, the voice was at its loudest. It seemed to be coming from…I walked from one wall to another, until finally I came to the one that adjoined the neighbouring unit. After some hesitation, I leaned in. The paint felt deathly cool against my cheek.

I closed my eyes.

I nearly jumped when someone tapped me on the shoulder. It was Terence, looking deservedly sheepish.

"You…you hear what the voice is saying?" When I didn't answer, he began to look concerned. "You look really pale. Are you feeling okay?"

I straightened up, feeling slightly dazed. My hands were clammy, and my lips felt numb. "I think I know what's going on."

—⁓—

"You clear on what you are supposed to do?"

Terence nodded uncertainly. "And what are *you* going to do?"

"I'm going over to your next-door neighbour. Say hello. Chit-chat."

He looked incredulous. "Come on, tell—"

"Quick," I admonished, pushing him towards the door. I glanced at my watch—it was nearly eleven in the morning. "The HDB office will only be open till noon since it's a Saturday. Hurry." He complied obediently.

On Terence's living room table, I laid out a tape measure, notebook and pen I had earlier requisitioned from amongst the odds and ends that were scattered about the apartment. My neck was stiff. The voice in the night had died down eventually, and the two of us had decided to act like grown-ups and go back to sleep. But I didn't sleep well. I had dreams—murky dreams I couldn't recall. I was glad when I finally opened my eyes to a room bathed in the warm glow of the late morning sun.

Now, seeing that all that I was going to need was ready, I set out for the neighbour's.

Luckily for me, he was a friendly elderly man who hadn't the faintest clue as to what I was up to. After I introduced myself as his new neighbour, he warmly invited me into his flat. Many young people like me, he said, simply didn't have the neighbourliness of old, or *kampung* spirit, anymore. The previous occupants had never bothered to introduce themselves, much less engage in any sort of conversation. He knew next to nothing about them.

I was slightly disappointed to hear that, but the main purpose of my visit remained. I did feel a tingle of guilt, though, for his words rang true. But there was little time for that. I steered the small talk towards my topic of choice, the interior floor areas of HDB flats. Most of the new BTOs nowadays, I complained, were too small to be comfortable. That was the reason I had decided on getting a resale unit instead.

He nodded his head vigorously. A veritable chicken coop, that's what new flats were nowadays, he said. He had seen his children's new homes.

I swooped in. Would he mind, I asked, if I were to just take a quick measurement of his living room floor space? My friend, I lied, thought that I had gotten lucky with my unit. He didn't believe that all the four-room flats in this block were equally spacious. I had to prove him wrong.

The old man guffawed. Our units were practically mirror images of each other. The measurements would tally, down to the nearest millimetre. Go ahead, he said, waving his hand, see for yourself.

And so I made my way back to Terence's apartment, where I picked up the tape measure, notebook and pen I had at the ready. I wanted to smile, for everything had gone according to plan. But I could only bite my lip nervously.

"So," I said, when Terence was back from his trip to the HDB office, "what did you find out?"

"No alterations have been done to my flat previously. But I could have told you that. The previous owner told me as much."

I waved a dismissive hand. "We had to check to be sure. Now, I need you to call a contractor."

Terence looked at me, completely flummoxed. "A contractor? I thought we should be calling an exorcist or something, or at least a feng shui master."

"You heard me. Just do it. I'll explain later."

He gave a resigned sigh and reached into his pocket for his phone. "When shall I ask them to come down?"

"Today. ASAP."

"Bro, today is Saturday leh."

I gave a cluck of impatience. "Just offer to pay them more."

"But what do you even want them to do?"

I told him. He looked staggered. "You're kidding, right? Eh, seriously, tell me what the hell is going on."

I didn't reply. I could feel my stomach churning.

He pursed his lips. "I'm not going to do it unless I know what this is about."

"Fine," I said, pulling the trump card from up my sleeve. "You can spend tonight alone in your flat then. Ought to be fun."

With a sour face, he made the call.

—⁓—

The workmen shuffled their dirty boots uncomfortably as the contractor looked at Terence and me impatiently. Terence stared at his living room floor tiles, then at the dirty boots, then back at his floor. I looked at the tools they'd brought. They would do.

But first, I couldn't resist a touch of theatrics.

"Gentlemen," I said, "we are gathered here today because a deed most foul has been committed in this place. We are going to put it right."

The workmen, all of them foreigners from Bangladesh, looked at me without comprehension.

The contractor said: "Eh, can hurry up or not? I have to pay them extra for working today."

I ignored him. "This living room," I said, "measures 10.5 metres by 7 metres. The unit next door, which is supposed to be of exactly the same dimensions, measures 10.5 metres by 7.5 metres. That's half a metre unaccounted for."

They looked at me expectantly.

"My friend went down to the HDB office to make some enquiries. No major alterations have ever been made to this unit. As you know, such alterations must be approved by HDB before they can be done. So, where did the missing space go?"

I walked over to the wall that adjoined the neighbouring unit. I slapped my palm on it with a loud *thwack*. "See how much this wall actually protrudes into the living room. An unauthorised alteration has been made." Turning to the contractor, I said, "Mr Tan, could you get your men to hack it down, please?"

"Woah, woah, woah." Terence put his hand up in alarm. "How can you be so sure about that?"

"Ask him," I said simply, pointing at the contractor. He walked over to the wall in question and began to examine it closely. He rapped his knuckles against it to hear the sound it returned. He got down on all fours and scrutinised the line where the wall met the floor. He got up, brushed the dust off his hands, and nodded.

"Confirm false wall. More solid than normal false walls, but I quite sure."

The blood drained from Terence's face.

As the sledgehammers swung into the wall, raining plaster and wood flecks all about us, my friend and I stood in the far corner, fingers in ears, nerves on edge. "Why the hell did he build it?" Terence yelled over the din, but I pretended I couldn't hear him.

The work stopped abruptly, and silence hung in the air for a second.

"What? What is it?" I shouted, my heart thumping so hard I could hear the echo in my ears.

A babble of foreign syllables broke out as some of the workmen hurriedly took a step back while others surged forward with necks craned in curiosity. Gasps, then shouts. Yet a few more men stumbled back, holding their noses. One worker bravely rose above the confusion and, sledgehammer in hand, swung firmly at an unbroken spot at eye-level. Paint and debris flew. One more slam, and a pair of frenzied hands scrabbled to claw away the remaining loose chips.

A wizened brown face peered back at us, eyes closed, mouth open in a frozen scream. Its skin, stretched agonisingly taut over the skull, was leathery and raddled—not with age, but by death's savage hand.

Strangely, no one screamed. Even now I can remember Terence's face, a white petrified mask. The only thought that ran through my mind was how ridiculously small the head of the corpse looked, dry as a bone and all shrivelled up. Reality hit us only when the smell did, and the two of us clambered out of there almost on all fours.

Then things happened. I'm sorry, but I really can't get more specific than that. The police came. Paramedics, even—don't ask me who called them. Sanity only returned to us when Terence and I were back at my place, after scrubbing ourselves raw in the shower and changing into clean clothes. The police came over to ask us questions, lots of questions. They had some answers too. Turned out the previous owner's wife had left him after all—for another man. They conjectured that he had found out about her affair and, after killing her in a fit of rage, come up with a rather innovative method of hiding the body.

"How did you know she was in there?" the inspector asked with a rather nasty gleam of suspicion in his eye.

I was too frazzled to even try to lie. I told him about the voice we had heard that night, how I had put my ear to the wall and finally heard the words the ghostly voice had to say.

Please, I'm inside the wall.

"My god!" I cried, recoiling at the thought that had just struck me. "S-she wasn't still alive when, when I heard her, was she?"

"Decomposition of the body tells us that she's been dead for at least a few months," the officer said dryly. "And that pretty much puts the lie to your story too. Luckily for you, I'm inclined to think that it's the shocking discovery of the corpse that has muddled your memory. I'll be back again, and when I am, I expect nothing but the truth from you." After throwing me a most severe look, he left.

So that's it. Terence sold the house as quickly as he could, and thereafter he wrote to his Member of Parliament to appeal to IRAS to have the Seller's Stamp Duty waived. Which they did, "in view of the extraordinary circumstances", as their letter went, if I remember correctly.

There's been a question that I've been hounding Terence about ever since, but not once has he given me a straight answer.

Did he or did he not tell the subsequent buyer that the flat was haunted?

THE ELIXIR

"It's arrived," James said, poking his head through the door.

"Great," Shu Lin said. "Get it prepped. Oh, and remember, keep this whole thing quiet. The Chinese government wants it under wraps."

Her subordinate nodded and left. She wondered if he had managed to pick up on the excitement she tried so hard to conceal. That was what she hated about the promotion, having to wear the mask of the boss, the unflappable superior. The days of James and her bantering around were gone. They sure weren't kidding when they said it was lonely at the top.

But for the moment at least, there was a pleasant distraction. Her hand crept to the bottom drawer of her desk, from which she retrieved a thick stack of photographs and notes that had arrived a week earlier. Even in the photographs the ancient artefact exuded an air of mystery—and yes, also a sense of ominous dread. She could only wonder how it would feel to finally be able to touch the object itself, to examine its contents. To feel the centuries fall away as antiquity collided with present day with a simple touch of her finger. It was too much for any one person to bear.

She had no idea how she'd been able to keep a lid on her bubbling excitement all this while. From the moment they reached out to her—out of the blue—she couldn't quite bring herself to believe it. Really, why would the Chinese government entrust such a precious find to a Singapore government research agency, renowned as it might be? But she was beginning to understand now. The discovery wasn't just a momentous one. It was stupendous. There was no way the Chinese could have kept out inquisitive noses had they sent the artefact to any one of their own excellent research institutes or universities. But here in Singapore, they could expect a certain amount of…*discretion*.

There was a knock on the door, and it opened before she could even say "Come in". It was Prof Jennings, grinning from ear to ear. "A little bird told me it's here," he crooned.

She nodded, trying to hide her irritation. The stout, middle-aged man was an esteemed archaeologist visiting from a prestigious American university, and as reluctant as she'd been, there had been no way to keep him out of this. She needed his expertise.

The professor rubbed his hands in glee. "A mummy, can you believe it. A real-life mummy. I sure hope this one has a fabulous curse."

—⁓—

The stately sarcophagus lay in the dead centre of the room. There was a reverent hush, almost as if someone very important—a present-day someone, that is—was dead. Eyes followed them as she and Prof Jennings slowly approached the sand-coloured stone coffin. She could feel the man's impatience and excitement bristling, and she knew if they weren't being watched by so many pairs of eyes, he would rush past her like a boy to the new gaming machine at the arcade.

The foot of the sarcophagus was pointing towards them, the lid already removed but the mummy not yet in view. The coffin had high sides—a metre or so, she estimated—and it sat on a number of trestles, so it was impossible to see what it contained until one was practically standing beside it. She could feel her own heart racing now. The photos had only shown the exterior of the sarcophagus and not its contents. As a biochemical researcher, she had never had a mummy come to her for study, and she could only imagine what it would look like. Surely not too different from the Egyptian ones, she thought, since the preservation techniques used couldn't have been that different. Swaddled in bandages, with just some streaks of leathery skin peeking out here and there.

Almost there. If she tiptoed she could probably see it. Prof Jennings, unable to contain himself any longer, darted forward. Craning his neck, he let out an awed sigh. He leaned over, his hands falling atop the thick sides of the sarcophagus to support himself—whether breathless from the excitement or to take a closer look, she didn't know.

"Careful!" cried a voice in Mandarin. An arm in a white lab coat shot out to restrain the animated professor. It belonged to a distinguished-looking gentleman of around 60 or so, whose face was now twisted with grave concern—and exertion, as he struggled to hold on to the professor who was doing his best to escape his grasp. From his appearance and demeanour, Shu Lin guessed that he was Prof Li, the Chinese government official she'd been liaising with on the matter.

"Professor Jennings!" she cried, leaping forward, keenly aware of the disapproving murmurs behind her. "Let's not get overexcited."

She gasped. The mummy...didn't look like a mummy at all. In fact, she couldn't even be sure it was a corpse at first. The woman was *beautiful*, and the condition of her body was nearly pristine. She was completely submerged in a clear liquid, and the interplay of the spotlights in the room and the fluid lent her face an ethereal, tranquil glow. Really, she might as well be in the middle of a bath or something (clothes on, of course)—she seemed that alive. The frayed and faded palatial finery that she was clad in only served to set off her youth…her *sparkle*.

"What the hell," she mumbled, staggered at the sight.

"It's marvellous, simply marvellous." Prof Jennings had somehow slipped free from the grip of the other man, but somewhat chastened, he kept his hands tucked behind the small of his back, choosing only to lower his face so close to the surface of the liquid that his nose was almost touching.

The elderly Prof Li faced the two of them solemnly. With a slight bow, he intoned, in English this time, "May I present to you, Lady Yun Feng, Emperor Hsu's most favoured concubine!"

———

"He wants *what*?"

"The whole team gone. Only you to remain," James said, shrugging his shoulders slightly in the way he always did when he had to convey bad news.

"That's ridiculous. Where is he? I'm going to speak to him right now."

"In the room."

She left her office in a huff. There was no need to ask which room—for now, and probably the next few months to come, there would only be one room of interest.

"Prof Li," she said, flinging open the door. "You can't just—"

"Good morning, Director. I have been eagerly expecting you." His voice was calm and smooth, unhurried. "I am very sorry to have asked your team to leave the room, but I assure you that it is completely necessary."

"I need my team in order to do the work, to help you."

"I have no doubt that you alone are more than qualified to help me with what I need."

"No matter how qualified, I can't do everything by myself. I *need* my team," she repeated, clasping an emphatic hand on his arm for good measure. *Not to mention that I haven't handled a test tube in, what, years?* That was the price of climbing through the ranks. You put aside the things you originally set out to do to, instead, do things your superiors saw as important.

The old man shook his head slowly. "You can take all the time you need, Director. But this matter is of the utmost delicacy. My superior, in fact, is quite upset that so many were present when the mummy was first unveiled. He very nearly wanted to call the whole thing off. I had to beg him to change his mind."

Just who is your superior anyway? she wanted to ask, for despite the thick curtains of bureaucracy she'd had to deal with, Prof Li had been her only point of contact. It frustrated her, knowing there had to be hundreds, thousands of wheels spinning in the background, just out of sight, but being privy only to what was deemed suitable for her eyes. There were so many questions she wanted to ask about the sarcophagus and its contents, but no other Chinese contact of hers knew about it at all, or so they all claimed. Lady Yun Feng they knew of, but as far as they were aware, her remains were never found. Either the matter was really a well-kept secret, kept within the confines of officialdom, or the Chinese government was really putting the pressure on the scholarly community to stay mum on the issue.

"Let me put together a special team for this. Only consisting of the most dependable, trustworthiest people."

"Director, I've already told you—"

"These are my terms, Prof Li. I'm sorry, but there is no way I can work alone on this matter. If the Chinese government is unable to accept my terms, I'm afraid you'll have to look elsewhere."

She held her breath. Had she been too hasty in issuing the ultimatum? But she didn't have a choice.

If she was going to do this, she was going to do this properly, with a properly qualified team. Anything else would only bring the agency—and her—to disrepute. She had worked too damn hard to reach the top to have an old stubborn foreign official tarnish her name simply because he was paranoid about secrecy.

He was studying her very carefully, as if wondering if he should call her bluff. There was a sharp, shrewd gleam in his eye, the culmination, she knew, of decades and decades of dealing with people just like her—and himself. But she knew he didn't have much of a bargaining chip, not with his ridiculous requirements. Where else could he go to? No self-respecting scientist would be willing to take on this immense task by her lonesome. The only advantage he held was that she badly wanted this, but if she had to guess, he, for some reason, wanted it to be her agency—or to be precise, *her*—just as badly.

He held up three fingers. Was he conceding?

"Just three of you in the team. Including yourself."

She nodded.

———

"The usual protocol is to submit the mummified remains to a suite of non-invasive diagnostic techniques such as X-rays and MRIs to determine the cause of death. In the present instance, we may encounter some difficulty doing that due to fluid the remains are immersed in. It will quite likely interfere with any procedure we attempt." Prof Jennings cleared his throat importantly. "I therefore propose that we first drain the fluid and store it separately for later analysis."

Try as she might, Shu Lin found it difficult to focus with the *thing* in the room. She had suggested to the others that they take the discussion to another room, but none of them would have it. Her eyes constantly strayed to the stone coffin, in which the corpse— yes, it was so fresh that she couldn't properly call it a mummy—lay. She couldn't get the image out of her mind: the beautiful, pristine features, kept perfect through the centuries, untouched by time and decay. Didn't any of the rest find it disconcerting in the slightest?

Prof Li was nodding at Jennings's words. "In fact," he said, "I would like to make it known that the priority of the Chinese government is the fluid itself, not the remains. There is reason to believe that the fluid may have certain...*unique* properties."

No shit, Sherlock, she thought. *Any idiot could tell you that no known liquid has preservational properties close to that.*

Jennings's head was pumping up and down furiously. "Quite so, quite so. There is every indication that the fluid is quite unlike anything ever studied by archaeologists. Quite honestly, this find is *groundbreaking*, and I really think we should be bringing in more experts on this."

Li opened his mouth to protest, but Shu Lin forestalled him: "Thank you, Professor Jennings, but for now I think the Chinese government has made it clear that it prefers for the matter to be confined to as few personnel as possible. And our agency will respect that." The American harrumphed mutinously, but she had her trump card. "In any case, I suspect that bringing in more experts may…*dilute* the credit due to our esteemed visiting archaeologist in the event of any discovery. I'm quite anxious to avoid that." She gave him her most winning smile and grinned inwardly as the diminutive figure straightened and puffed his chest. There was no further protest heard.

A little more discussion and it was agreed that since the fluid was the priority, they would take a sample of it for testing before deciding how best to drain and store it. They would take no unnecessary risks until more was known about it—for all they knew it could be incredibly toxic, or flammable. James would take on the task. She knew no other biochemist who was more conscientious and knowledgeable in the field, but more than that, he was someone she could trust. She had never had such a small team before—just she, James and Jennings—but his presence comforted her.

All eyes were on James as the tip of the pipette slid gingerly into the fluid—and here, Shu Lin had to admit, she half expected the glass to start smoking on contact—and after a second or two, when no reaction was observed, James released the plunger with a smooth, practised motion of his thumb, and the clear liquid shot up the shaft. The sample was promptly deposited into a test tube, and everyone heaved a sigh of relief as the tube was stoppered and bagged by the scientist's steady gloved hands. He winked at Shu Lin, a boyish grin breaking out on his face. He used to do that back when they still shared a lab together, she remembered. She found herself smiling back.

"All right, off to work I go," he said and, with a swish of his lab coat, disappeared through the door.

—⁓—

The four figures sat placidly around the table, emitting faint groans as they stared at what remained of dinner.

"Finish the last slice, someone," Shu Lin said, waving a weak hand at the last open pizza box. On one side of it rose a pile of empty boxes, stacked several storeys high. No one moved.

"How long more?" she asked, turning to James.

He looked at his watch. "At least another hour, probably. I've got to check on them in a bit." He looked around the room. "You all go on home first. It's late. No need to wait for me."

Again, no one moved. They weren't waiting for him, but for the machines whirring away in the next room, teasing out the individual compounds of the unknown fluid. Waiting for the answer that they were all dying to know.

"It's all right, James. I don't think anyone is going anywhere." She closed the lid on the forlorn last slice of pizza. "Anyone up for dessert? There's some mooncake in the pantry fridge."

Li and James shook their heads, and the latter rose. "I'm going to check on the chromatography. It should be almost done by now."

"What's mooncake?" Jennings asked lazily, one hand on his heaving hump of a belly.

"Some kind of Chinese pastry. Sweet. Want to try?"

"Don't mind if I do."

Shu Lin headed for the pantry. When she returned, she found the American listening closely as the Chinese professor regaled his one-man audience with the origins of the delicacy she held in her hands. "Fascinating, fascinating," he said, his eyebrows wiggling appreciatively. "Ah, and here comes the Moon Goddess with some mooncake."

"I see you've been telling the good professor about the legend of Chang'e. She placed the plate before Jennings. "Which version did you tell him?"

"My, my, how many versions *are* there?"

"Several," Li said, smiling. "I told him the one where the archer Hou Yi shot down nine suns and gained the elixir of immortality as a reward, only to have his apprentice Peng Meng try to steal the gift of everlasting life from his master."

"And Hou Yi's wife, Chang'e, drank the elixir herself in a desperate bid to stop the thief," Shu Lin continued. "Upon drinking it, she gained immortality and flew off to the moon."

Li nodded.

She smiled. "I've always preferred the other version. More tragic, but also closer to reality, I think."

The Chinese professor laughed. Jennings simply looked puzzled.

"In the other story, it starts off the same. Hou Yi the archer shoots down nine of the ten suns, doing the people a great service. In return, they made him king. But the throne soon made him an arrogant man, so much so that he dared ask for the elixir of immortality from the Queen Mother of the West, who acceded to his demand. All this while, Chang'e had been watching with wary eyes as her husband's reign grew increasingly tyrannical. She knew that if her husband were to drink the elixir and gain immortality, the people would suffer. So when the elixir arrived, she beat Hou Yi to the punch and drank it before he could. She flew off to the moon, staring down sadly at her husband, a man she had once loved, a man who had once been honourable. The king, in a fit of rage, picked up his bow and fired a shot at the fast-receding figure. But she was already immortal, and the arrow could do her no harm."

Li roared with laughter. "Quite a bit of embellishment there, Director."

Shu Lin shrugged and smiled wryly. "I may have projected some of the horror stories I've heard from my divorcee friends."

Jennings wasn't listening to either of them. His eyes had a faraway look, and he was muttering to himself. "Fascinating! Chang'e could very well be the first feminist figure in Chinese mythology."

"What's *her* story, Professor Li?" she asked, pointing at the sarcophagus. Its presence still disquieted her, but spending hours with it at such close quarters had a way of blunting its effect.

Li grew serious at the question. Even Jennings must have noticed the change in the mood of the room, for he snapped out of his reverie and turned to the Chinese professor expectantly. When Li spoke, it seemed that he was picking his words one by one, as if careful not to depart from the official narrative.

"Strictly speaking, we don't know a lot about Lady Yun Feng. As I mentioned previously, she is believed to be Emperor Hsu's favourite concubine. The circumstances of her death are not found in the historical records as far we are aware, but there is plenty of speculation. Many believe she died young, from an illness the royal physicians were unable to treat. From what we can observe of the body right now, that would certainly appear to be a plausible hypothesis."

There was a clear "but..." lingering in the air.

"What is *your* personal view on the matter, Professor?" Shu Lin ventured.

The elderly man looked hesitant. "Well," he said, "it is really no more than mere surmise on my part..."

Their gazes did not falter.

He sighed. "There is a footnote in the annals, a small footnote, to be sure, overlooked or ignored by most historians. The emperor was displeased with the concubine, although the reason for his displeasure was never specified. This happened close to the time she died, so I'm surprised that not more scholars are putting two and two together, as you might say."

"You think he had her killed?"

"It is quite possible, don't you think? Not executed publicly, of course, but that is hardly the only way he could have gone about it. Poisoned, I would guess, going by the state of her body."

"But why go through that trouble, when he could have just ordered her killed like any other person who displeased him?"

Li looked solemn, almost severe. "Usually, there is only one reason why the emperor would have someone killed off in secret. Because the offence, if brought to light, would bring embarrassment upon him or the royal family."

Jennings looked as if he had a question or remark on his lips, but before he could even utter a word, James had burst through the door.

"My god, guys, you have to hear this."

The room was deathly quiet.

"The chromatography was done. The fluid contains just two different components. Now, from handling the fluid it is quite clear that the fluid is a water-based mixture, so one of them is almost certainly water. I ran the other substance through the spectrometer, and get this—the result was inconclusive."

"Human error, of course," piped up Jennings, and this immediately earned him a withering glare from the scientist.

"I considered that possibility, *obviously*. As unlikely as it was. So I ran it through the spectrometer again. And again. Each time, it was the same result. Inconclusive."

"But this means…" the Chinese professor looked pale. "Impossible…"

"It's an unknown element or isotope." Shu Lin stood up, her voice firm. "Of course, we'll need to have another team confirm the results, but for now I think we can proceed on the assumption that we are dealing with something that mankind has never before encountered." She felt a thrill run through her skin—a feeling at once familiar and alien, like a long-forgotten smell from childhood. It had been too long since the last time she was on the brink of a significant discovery, but this—this was beyond significant. This was probably going to be world-changing. And she was right in the middle of it all.

She stared at the faces surrounding her. James was grinning madly, like he always did when something excited him. Jennings looked as though he might faint—Shu Lin realised with amusement, and a little concern, that every quivering breath of his was actually two or three separate, rapid intakes of breath. Prof Li—now that was strange—he was smiling, but his expression was strained, as if he was trying hard to maintain his composure, to hide his true feelings. The corners of his eyes and mouth seemed to twitch under the impetus of some intense emotion.

"Prof Li, are you all right?"

"Yes, yes, of course. This—this is simply astounding news, and I think I must report back at once."

"I think I need to do the same," Shu Lin said, smiling. "That said, I think we should all go back for some much-needed rest. Go on, everyone, I'll lock up after you. There's plenty of work to be done tomorrow."

Amidst hearty congratulations and pats on the back, the group rose and straggled out of the room. But Prof Li hovered behind, clearly wanting to catch a word in private with her.

Once they were alone, a gnarled hand shot out and grasped hers. She winced—he was surprisingly strong. "Director," he said urgently, "I am sorry to have to ask you this, but how confident are you that the analysis was conducted without…without human error?"

"As sure as I would be had I conducted it myself." Her voice was cool. "I'm honoured you sought us out for assistance, but now that you have, surely you might wish to place a little more confidence in our abilities."

"But an *unknown* element!" he hissed, and Shu Lin thought she saw a flash of fury in his eyes. "Do you really expect me to believe that?"

"I expect you to believe whatever the evidence leads us to believe, Professor," she said, unceremoniously twisting her hand from his. "As I would of any reasonable person."

The professor's eyes narrowed. He leaned in, putting his face close to hers. She stared back, unflinching and unmoving.

"Be careful not to get too insolent, young lady. You do not yet comprehend the full seriousness of the matter."

"Perhaps I would, if you had been kind enough to explain it."

His head snapped back, almost as if he had been slapped. Standing ramrod straight, he stared down at her imperiously, face red and chest heaving. "I see that our relationship has deteriorated to the point where we are no longer able to work together. As such, I am withdrawing from this collaboration at once. Kindly release the artefact to me without further ado."

"Very well. First thing tomorrow I shall make arrangements for the artefact to be prepped and returned to the Chinese government."

"Good. I expect to receive it before the end of tomorrow."

"Don't be ridiculous, Professor. It took us close to a month to make arrangements for the transportation of the artefact from your facility to ours. I think you should expect a similar lead time for the return journey. It's only reasonable."

He stiffened. His entire body, from his feet, to his torso, to his face, to the very lashes on his eyes, seemed to turn to stone. She found herself holding her breath, not daring to move.

"I CANNOT WAIT THAT LONG!" His eyes were wild, bloodshot, and his mien, having shaken off all pretence of restraint, was now utterly under the sway of his emotions.

She took an involuntary step back from the outburst. The dispassionate part of her, the scientist, marvelled—from a distance—at the sudden and complete transformation from genteel official to raving madman. The other parts of her tensed and prepared for the worst.

"Is everything okay in here?" It was James, thank god, his head poking around the door as he alternated his concerned glance between her and the professor, who by now had, rather remarkably, purged all anger from his expression and voice.

"Yes, everything is fine. Regrettably, Professor Li has seen it fit to withdraw the Chinese government's request for our help. He was just leaving."

James raised his eyebrows but said nothing.

Shu Lin pulled the door wide open, firmly. "Will you be kind enough to show the professor out?"

"Please," the official said stiffly, now all poise and rectitude, "I will show myself out."

The door slammed after him, leaving James staring at his boss in bewilderment. "What the hell?"

Shu Lin shrugged. "I guess I was afraid this would happen sooner or later. He wasn't exactly someone easy to work with."

"But the discovery! My god, this was going to be the find of the century!"

She gave a small smile. "Don't worry, it still is. There's still leftover sample, isn't there?"

He nodded.

"First thing tomorrow, send it to a reputable independent lab overseas. We can't reveal the full provenance, but we can give them enough to make their own inferences. Nothing that will breach the non-disclosure, of course."

"But the Chinese government…"

"They'll have to live with it. We held up our end of the bargain; they didn't."

"All right." James sighed, then yawned. "Let's go, shall we? It's late."

"You go ahead. I have one more thing to do."

When James had left, she slowly made her way down the dark and silent corridor. Ridiculous as it was, she couldn't shake off the feeling that she was intruding…on someone's repose, as it were. With a small squeak of protest, the door opened to reveal the sarcophagus, gloomily illuminated by a solitary spotlight. The rest of the room was blanketed in shadow. Almost on tiptoe, she stole over. The open coffin was covered with a clear acrylic plate, and there *she* was, looking as resplendent as she did the first time they had all laid eyes on her.

"Yun Feng," she whispered, laying a soft hand on the acrylic. It felt warm, and in her heart she felt the blooming of an strange sense of kinship. "What did you do that made the emperor so angry he had you killed? Many would guess an affair, of course, because to many that's all a woman was capable of. Did you upstage him? Make him feel small?" She couldn't help the wry smile that alighted upon her lips as she thought about the many men who had treated her with such kindliness, such solicitude— until they discovered, to their horror, that she was smarter, more capable than they. Even James... She once thought that they had a shot at something special, but the day she pipped him to the director post, she knew—there was just this *look* in his eyes as he congratulated her—that any chance of that had turned to dust.

"Well, whatever it was, I'm not sure the emperor won." Her fingers danced slowly across the concubine's lovely face, tracing the exquisite features that had, impossibly, eluded the passage of the centuries. "I can only imagine how he must be now, mere dust in the earth. And look at you—as beautiful as you were on the day they buried you." Looking upon the ghostly visage, she tried to smile, but the tomb-like atmosphere in the room was beginning to gnaw away at the sense of camaraderie that had seemed so strong only moments ago. She was talking to a *corpse* after all, she realised. In her sudden haste to move away, she jogged one of the trestles, and the entire stone coffin shook—leaden, lumbering motions that threatened to overcome and upset the entire supporting apparatus. Desperately, she threw out her hands to steady what had turned into a massive stone rocking cradle, and she gasped as the sloshing liquid within, icy cold, slopped through and wet her hands. Her eyes tried anxiously to pierce the wild wavelets that shrouded the body, hoping against hope that the frail flesh wouldn't strike the sides of the coffin.

Her efforts seemed to be paying off. Yes, the lurching motions were slowing, there was no doubt about that. She watched, in relief, as the rippling on the liquid's surface began melting back into a calm smoothness.

Then a barely stifled scream escaped her mouth. It was all she could do to suppress the urge to run, the urge to let go of the still-heaving coffin.

It had blinked—hadn't it? The corpse. The eyelashes had twitched, and the eyes, with the barest of spasms, had opened infinitesimally—and closed again.

Hands shaking, she released her hold as soon as the sarcophagus had steadied, and reached for her racing heart. A trick of the light and the still-undulating surface, surely. *What, a corpse coming to life after centuries of being submerged in a liquid?* she scolded herself. *And me, a scientist too.*

This was crazy. The whole thing was driving her nuts—the centuries-old undecomposed body, the irate Chinese official, and the nearly twenty-four hours since she'd properly slept. She had to go home.

Grabbing her satchel, she left the room without giving the sarcophagus a second look. She couldn't.

At the exit, the security guard nodded at her as she approached. "Aiyoh, work till so late ah, Director."

She gave a wan smile. "Could you please lock up after me? I'm the last one to leave."

The guard looked puzzled. "Are you sure, ma'am? What about the old professor?"

"Old professor? You mean the *angmoh*?"

"No, no. The Chinese."

Her face stiffened. "He still hasn't left?"

He nodded. "I saw the *angmoh* and James—Mr Lim, I mean—leave, but not the old Chinese guy. Is everything o—"

But she was already gone.

—⁓—

It was like walking the cemetery at night. She felt her way down the dark corridor, half expecting, with every step, to bump into something—*someone*, she corrected herself. A particular someone, in fact, and boy was she going to give him hell when she found him. She now wished she had asked the guard to accompany her, but really, between his paunch and his smoker's lungs, she was probably better off on her own.

She thought she could hear a noise from a ways off. Her first instinct was to head for the laboratory, where all the expensive equipment was, but she reminded herself that she wasn't looking for a thief. Prof Li's interest all this while had been centred on the artefact, so…

She didn't really want to venture, again, into the room where the sarcophagus was, but it'd be a lot worse if anything happened to it while it was under her watch. Like if it went missing, for example. She didn't quite see the frail 70-something-year-old lugging the entire one-tonne-odd coffin out on his own, but he might very well be capable of lifting the concubine's petite form.

Her heart skipped a beat when she saw that the door to the room was slightly ajar. She had closed it properly, hadn't she? She was almost absolutely certain she had. She sidled up to the gap, careful to make no noise at all. Slowly, oh so slowly, she peered through the gap.

There he was. She swallowed hard. Her jaw tightened. And what the…The acrylic plate had been removed. He was bent over, back to her, and—she leaned in a little closer—oh yes, there were some strange noises. Splashing—no, slurping.

My god, what is that freak up to?

She tried to steel herself, but her knees insisted on being wobbly. Ignoring them, she slapped the door wide open and charged into the room.

"Just *what* do you think you're doing!" she bellowed.

The bowed figure froze—then whipped around with a frightening suddenness. She quailed at the sight. His eyes were bloodshot and frenzied, and his lips—still dripping with the clear liquid he had clearly been imbibing—twisted themselves into a savage snarl. He advanced, fists balled.

"Professor Li—" she began, only to duck aside desperately as he sprung towards her. But there was no escaping the vice-like grips that clamped down on her arms painfully, digging into her soft flesh. *That's what a mouse must feel*, rose a distant thought amidst the red-hot panic, *when an owl seizes it with its claws.* A moment of wild terror as she was driven through the air, her feet swept clean off the ground—then a flash of sharp pain and a shuddering gasp as she was slammed against the wall with a sickening crack. Her wiry assailant was much stronger than he looked.

"Why—must—you—*interfere!*" he screamed, firing flecks of spit right into her cowering face.

Her mind was working feverishly now. If she screamed, the guard just might hear her, but who knew what that maniac might do to her while her knight in baby blue huffed and heaved himself to her rescue? *Remember your self-defence classes*, she implored her brain.

"W-why are you doing this, P-Professor?" she somehow managed, despite the bony arm that had by now wedged itself against her throat.

"*Why!*" Wisps of thin grey hair, loose from his carefully pomaded pate, twisted about indignantly in his hot breath. "Do you know who *I* am? And yet worms like you disrespect me, are incapable of fulfilling the smallest of my wishes!"

He's mad. Totally bonkers. Keep him talking.

"You know what she was?" His finger, ramrod straight, trembling slightly, was pointing at the sarcophagus now. "A mere kitchen maid," he spat. "She was *nothing, nothing* before I took her as *my* concubine. And how does she repay my kindness? By nearly robbing me of my immortality. That's right"—he leaned into her face, leering—"turns out your little Chang'e story had more to it than you realised, eh?"

He removed his arm from her throat, and she was down on the ground, gasping. For breath, and also... His story was ludicrous, of course, but try as she might she couldn't shake the image of the concubine's face, encased in immortal youth...

"Thousands upon thousands of men and horses I had sent far and wide, in search of the elixir of life.

And when they had at last found it, what does this whore do? She took it for herself. Oh, yes, she did." His scoff of disbelief quickly twisted into a demented grin. "She had no idea, of course, that there was plenty where it came from—plenty. And so the punishment had to fit the crime. Since she wanted the elixir so badly, she would have all she wanted— and more. She would *bathe* in it." He was laughing hard, with the abandon of a madman. "And best of all, because of the elixir she'd drunk, because of the elixir she was immersed in, she couldn't die, you see. Oh, you should have seen the first year—how she struggled, how she fought! I had to post four strong guards by her side the entire time, to hold her down. But eventually she seemed to fall into a deeper sleep of some sort, even though my physicians assured me she was very much alive."

She wasn't really listening anymore. Instead, her gaze crept to the stone coffin, where any moment now she expected a wet hand to reach out and grab the side. A part of her didn't want to believe the story. But the other part reminded her that they hadn't checked for vital signs—why would anyone have, in the first place? An eternity of drowning. The man was a monster.

"And so I had her entombed, to suffer forever. Having now drunk the elixir myself, I had the fountain where it came from destroyed. Impulsive, I know.

That has always been my shortcoming. But why should I share this glorious gift with those who are undeserving?" He laughed ruefully. "I couldn't have known that its effect wasn't permanent. And when I did realise it, hundreds of years later, when I found the lines on my face deepening, my vitality draining from me, I knew I had to act. I tried drinking from the elixir I had her submerged in, but it was clear that it had lost much of its potency. I had to find out how to make the elixir, fresh." His eyes were no longer wistful—they drilled right into her. "I came to you. You were supposed to be the best. But I should have known better than to seek help from a woman. Look where it got me."

"So there is no Chinese government behind you. It's just—just you," she spat.

"*Just* me?" he roared, closing in on her. She cowered, drawing her knees in, but he only pressed in further. "All China was once mine."

He screamed as her stilettoed foot shot up into the air, stabbing him square in the crotch. She was up on her feet, and throwing all her weight forward, she shoved him—right into the waiting sarcophagus behind him. There was an almighty crash, almost as if the entire room was collapsing into itself.

She got to her feet unsteadily. Her head was still a bit fuzzy from the impact, and she didn't know what she was seeing at first. She saw the professor, floundering around wildly, and for a moment she thought it was because of the massive slab of stone pinning down his legs—until she saw the pale hands wrapped around his neck, squeezing so tightly the knuckles gleamed under the spotlight.

It took her nearly a minute to snap out of the spell.

She had just closed the door behind her when a familiar figure appeared at the end of the corridor. He was clearly out of breath. "What happened, ma'am? I heard a loud noise. Everything okay?"

She gave him a bashful smile. "That was me, I'm afraid. I was really clumsy and knocked over a chair."

His nose twitched in suspicion.

She put a firm hand on his shoulder. "Really, it's fine. There might be a bit of a mess, but I'll be back tomorrow to deal with it."

"The Chinese gentleman?"

She shrugged. "No sign of him. I must be mistaken."

It barely took a second for him to decide that his paltry salary wasn't worth him asking any questions, especially when it was the director herself saying that everything was fine. He nodded and smiled. "Good night, Director."

"Good night."

Once he was out of sight, she calmly turned around. Opening the door just a crack, she peered in, like a concerned mother checking on her child.

For a moment she simply stood and looked on, her smile almost maternal.

Then, with a sigh, she closed the door with a soft, sharp click, but in the dead of the night she thought it sounded just like the doors of judgment slamming shut.

THE LAST GOODBYE

I was just about to turn in when I received the SMS from Leon.

Could you come over? he asked.

It's nearly 11, I replied. *I've got work tomorrow.* It was a little weird, to be honest. I mean, yes, I'd been to his place before, had drinks late into the night even, but this was totally different.

His reply came quickly: *Please, if you can. Please.* Desperation just brings out the worst in me. I ignored his message and went to brush my teeth. When I returned I saw that I had five missed calls. From Leon, of course.

"Dude, what the hell is wrong with you?" I said, when he picked up after the first ring.

"Oh, thank god you called back. Can you come over, please? Just a while. It won't take long, I promise."

"I'm not going anywhere until you tell me what this is about."

"Please—I-I'm in trouble. Really deep trouble. I need to talk to someone, Joel. Please."

I sighed. "Give me fifteen minutes."

I suppose I was being rather harsh. Most people wouldn't treat their childhood friends like that, even less so if they were still in close contact. You see, Leon and I were colleagues. Mere coincidence—I, for one, don't like mixing friendship with work. Friendship can complicate matters at work sometimes, especially if you're looking to climb. Especially if you're both looking to climb.

As I sped down the near-empty Central Expressway towards Leon's flat in Ang Mo Kio (seriously, that guy actually still lived at his parents' place), my mind wandered. Leon didn't have a habit of getting into trouble. He had no vices—save for drinking, and I suspect that's only because his friends drank—had no wife, no girlfriend. Maybe the odd fling or two with the girls in his department, but I have a funny feeling that he only brought them out to dinner, nothing more. He hadn't changed that much from secondary school, really. We used to laugh at him all the time, though we allowed him to tag along. Just the same way heroes tolerated their idiot sidekicks, I suppose. Quite mean of us, really, but you know what teenagers are like.

As I turned into his HDB estate, I grimaced slightly at the sight. Even in the dark, the dense columns of off-white blocks stood out gauchely. I never understood why he had never moved out, especially after his parents passed away. It certainly wasn't the money—heck, he earned more than I did, as much as I hated to admit it. As the VP of Sales and Distribution, he was probably the most senior guy at the bank still living in public housing. It's totally ridiculous.

As I stepped into the lift I glanced at my watch: 11.20 p.m. I wasn't going to stay longer than an hour. He might be my senior at work, but he wasn't from the same department. Heck, even if he was...some guys like Leon just don't rise above the pecking order of their youth, no matter how old or successful they get.

His flat was in a corner, all the way down the corridor. The windows were dark. I wondered if, after all that fuss, he had perhaps fallen asleep. I rang the doorbell, appreciating how its sharp twang cut through the silence of the night. A slight to-do inside—a door swinging open, the thudding of footsteps—and the front door opened a little to reveal a pale, glistening face.

"Thanks for coming, Joel." He stared at me with that pleading look in his eyes that I thoroughly detested, still hunkering behind the door as if he was on the lookout for some unseen enemy.

I waited for a few seconds, saying nothing. Then, realising he had no intention of moving, I walked up the steps and pushed the door wide open to let myself in, heaving against the weight of the man. The bottom of the door must have caught his toes, for he gave a yelp of pain and hopped away holding one foot. I did my best not to chuckle.

He must have been in bed, or at least getting ready for it, for he was wearing pyjamas—yes, actual pyjamas: a shiny silk polka-dotted long-sleeved shirt and matching bottoms. I swear, sometimes he reminds me of Mr Bean.

"What the hell, man. You wear that to sleep?" I said. The inside of his home was dim, but I knew, from experience, that his face was lighting up like a tomato at my words. "Can you switch on the lights or something?"

One hand still holding on to his foot, he scrabbled against the wall until he found the switch. The living room, awash in harsh white light, was a familiar sight. Many a drinking session and poker night had been had here, from the time we were in the army to just a few weeks back, when Ben, our mutual friend, made a killing at the poker table—at Leon's expense. The whole place looked like it was still frozen in the early 2000s: a boxy, yellowed plasma TV that, even at its prime, couldn't have been considered state-of-the-art; a mahjong table, its felt already worn thin and sporting several gaping holes, that served as our poker table and doubled as a dining table for Leon's usual solitary dinner in front of the TV; and a sagging sofa that sat like a shapeless sack of mush against the wall. Frankly, if not for the fact that poker night at Leon's also meant an open bar, I doubt any of us would have visited as often as we did.

"Seriously, man," I said, "it's really time you visited Ikea or something."

"Wha—" He started slightly before turning around and giving a rather foolish grin. "Oh…yes, yes, I suppose. It's comfortable, though."

I rolled my eyes.

There was a strange jumpiness about him, even by his standards. I waited for a moment or two, expecting him to start talking about why he had asked me over, but after a minute or two of silence, I knew he was just going to stare at me with those infuriatingly weak and slightly hopeful eyes until I said something.

"Well," I said, clucking my tongue in irritation, "what the hell is this about?"

He shifted his feet about uncomfortably.

"Come on man," I said, my voice rising, "it's late and I want to go home and sleep." I get angry when I'm uncomfortable, and there was something about the whole situation that gnawed at me, though I didn't know what. The company was bad, no surprises there, but there was something else. Perhaps it was the long silences, or just the oppressive air, but the longer I stood around the more my discomfiture grew.

"Can—can we talk inside my room?" he said, walking towards a closed door in an alcove beyond the living room. He opened the door slightly, allowing me to catch a glimpse of the dim confines behind the door. For some reason I felt a shiver run through me.

"Woah, woah, woah," I protested, holding out my hands. "That's too weird, man." It occurred to me that, despite all the times I'd been to his place, I had never once seen the inside of his bedroom. But what was stranger still was the primitive fear and repulsion that gripped my heart as I glanced inside. There was something about the darkness within— was it just fluttering curtains I saw, or something else? Or perhaps it was the desperate loneliness it reeked of that scared and repulsed me. Whatever it was, I couldn't help it.

"Oh, of course, sorry. We can just talk out here then."

I nodded, tapping my watch. 11.30 p.m. "Make it quick, dude."

He motioned at the sofa, and reluctantly I sat myself on the wobbly thing.

"I'm sorry to trouble you, Joel. I really am. But you're my best friend, always have been. Since we were kids."

I had to fight to keep the scorn from my eyes and lips. How could anyone be so blind?

"I think that's when it started. Since we were kids. I've never been *anyone*, you know. Never done anything worth noticing. I was a nobody. A loser, a worthless piece of shit. I know it. I knew it even back then. Oh yes"—he looked at me, smiling weakly through glistening eyes—"I knew what you guys were saying behind my back, but I was happy enough to be seen with you guys, you know? Happy enough to be taken notice of, even if it wasn't for anything good."

I was staggered. It's easy enough to mock someone behind his back, someone you think is so hopelessly clueless about everything, but when he turns around and looks you in the eye, you have to be cold, really cold, not to feel the slightest pang of remorse at all.

"Look, Leon," I said, shaking my head. "I'm sorry. We were young then."

"No, it's okay. I'm not looking for an apology, not at all. I'm just saying, that's how it started."

"What started, man?" I leaned back slowly, trying to edge away. Thinking back, we had been rather hard on him. He made it so easy because he never pushed back—ever. He just stood there and took it, always with that dazed look in his eyes and nervous half-smile. Had he finally cracked? Was he looking to…

"*This* started—looking at you guys, at others, wishing I had what it takes to be *somebody*. Not just a nameless loser trying to hang around with the cool kids. And you know, I thought it would get better when I started uni, but no. It was the same. That's when I realised—it would always be the same. You can't escape who you are. You can't be someone you're not."

"That's bullshit, dude. Look at you now. We all started at the same time, and you're more senior than any of us. You made it, man."

He shook his head sadly. "I'll come to that later." Taking a breath, he continued: "You remember the time in uni we both liked Chloe? Chloe from business faculty?"

It took a while, but I remembered. Only I hadn't really liked her, not really. She dressed up well and all that, but I'd thought she was rather plain. But Leon confided in me that he really fancied her, and well…old habits die hard, I guess. It took a few nice dinners and a walk or two on the campus grounds at night, but eventually I got what I wanted. And when I did, I dumped her. I know how it sounds like, but really, I…

"You dated her for a bit, Joel. I didn't blame you, not at all. All's fair in love and war and all that. But after you broke up, I thought I could have a shot with her, you know. I even asked you if it was okay."

Oh yes, he did. And, my god, I had snickered and said by all means.

"For weeks—months—I comforted her as she cried. Cried over you. Then she got better and eventually got over you. I finally built up the courage to ask her out. You remember that?"

I nodded. He had told me of his grand plan, a ridiculously elaborate scheme that involved a romantic dinner at a pricey restaurant and even a necklace. A mere acquaintance would have told him it was an awful idea, that it was bound to freak her out. But being the good friend that I was, I mentally rubbed my hands, prepped my popcorn and told him it was a good idea.

A deep sadness crept over his face. I closed my eyes and waited, bracing myself.

"She freaked out. She—she said—" his voice broke and tears rolled down his cheeks. I just looked at my hands. "She said I was a loser, and that she was insulted that I had even thought myself to be good enough."

She wasn't a nice girl, not at all, but I don't think I had helped things by telling her, while we dated, about Leon and how we basically kicked him around like a can.

"I, I— Look, I don't know what to say, but I'm really sorry. All that happened so long ago. Why can't you just let it go?"

"I'm not blaming you or anything, Joel. I'm really not. I just want to let you know how—why—I did what I did."

"And what the hell did you do, dammit!" I was sick of it, sick of being made to feel guilty, sick of being reminded how much of a douche I had been to him. If he wanted me to say sorry, fine, he could have all the apologies he wanted. All of that was in the past. He was successful now, even if he didn't know how to enjoy it. He had done better than any of us. So what more could he want?

"It happened during a trip overseas. A trip to— never mind, I'd rather not say. You'll soon see why." His voice was flat, lifeless, sounding very much like that of a criminal forced into a confession. "But the way I see it, it didn't have to be there. It could have happened anywhere."

"Look here, Leon." My shame had evaporated, leaving only resentment. "It's nearly midnight. I'm going to give you five minutes. Five minutes and I'm gone, okay?"

He grew white at my words. "It's nearly midnight?" He grabbed my hand and looked at my watch—and that was when I realised for the first time that there wasn't a single clock in the flat. "Fifteen minutes..." he whispered, his eyes wide with fear. "Please, please, Joel, don't go. I'll hurry." He licked his bloodless lips.

"The trip, it was a business trip, and I was just a lowly salesman for the bank then. I wasn't even in charge of the negotiations. Honestly I don't know why they even sent me. But I screwed up. I screwed up badly. So badly I probably sank the whole deal. Wrong words, wrong time. Typical me, of course. I knew I was going to lose my job. So that last day overseas, I was crying my eyes out in the hotel room. My roommate wasn't around. They'd left for 'R and R' as they called it, but since no one was in the mood to celebrate, it was probably more of a let's-bitch-about-Leon session.

"Something deep in my soul cried out. It wasn't just the screw-up, or the fear of losing my job. It was all those years of pent-up frustration, the self-loathing. The eternal urge of wanting to be more than I was that went unsatisfied, year after year. Finally it stared at me in the face. I couldn't pretend anymore. I was really a loser at life. And so I—I made a deal."

I raised my eyebrows. "Deal? With who?"

He shook his head and looked away.

I laughed tiredly. "What, you made a deal with the devil? Is that what you're saying?"

"This—is—*not*—a—joke," he hissed through clenched teeth. "Fuck you, Joel, fuck you."

I was going to protest, to hit back, but I saw something in his eyes that I'd never seen before, something that quelled me. For a moment I saw him in a dim hotel room, despairing and alone, his diminutive frame dwarfed by the darkness lurking around him, a sea of murmuring, undulating shadows waiting to swoop in for the kill.

"What did you do, Leon?" I whispered, the hair on my arm rising. "What the hell did you do?"

"I don't know, I don't know, I don't know," he bleated. His voice was so soft I could barely hear him; his breaths came faster, shallower. "I—I made some promises."

"To who?" I almost yelled.

"I don't know what it was!" he screamed, a fresh edge of panic rising in his voice. But midnight tonight, Joel, that is the time of reckoning. Ten years, I was given. And now—"

His composure completely crumbled, and he wept. "Now my time is up."

"Look here, man, look here," I said, licking my lips nervously. "This is just bullshit, all right? You were down and out, and your imagination just ran wild. This sort of thing happens only in stories."

"Really? What about the fact that when my team came back to the hotel that night, they were cheering and whooping. Somehow, the client had agreed to the deal, even though earlier in the day they'd more or less walked out on us out due to my blunder."

"These things can happen. Clients can be fickle as hell," I said, resisting the urge to look at my watch.

"It's not just that." His voice had gone back to being flat, stripped of emotion. "When I came back to Singapore, it was as if the universe now conspired to make me succeed. Sales leads rained down on me. Everyone was suddenly clamouring for me, even if previously they shunned me like the plague. I experimented, you know? Tried to screw up as much as possible. Said and did stupid things. But still the sales and commissions poured in. It was like I couldn't fail if I wanted to."

"You had a lucky break, that's all. A change in fortune…" I could barely hear myself, and I believed myself even less. It seemed unreal—ludicrous. Making a Faustian deal, selling one's soul—those belonged to the realm of imagination or the metaphorical. But as I sank deeper in my recollection of Leon's meteoric and unexpected rise, the uncanniness of it all became more and more apparent. Leon, with all the social skills of a potato, making a full VP in record time. *Didn't we whisper about it behind his back?* I asked myself. Made snarky remarks about how he had to be sleeping with the SVP or something, though we all knew that neither of them was gay. His explanation, as impossible as it was, seemed to make so much sense.

"It's all right, I suppose. For most of my life I've been nothing, and now I go back to nothing. But what lies beyond this life, Joel? That's what terrifies me. Please..." His eyes were fixed to my watch, unblinking. A minute to midnight.

On an inexplicable impulse my hand sprang forward to clutch his arm. "It'll be okay, Leon, it'll be okay," I said in barely above a whisper. I looked at his face, and it was like seeing a person I'd never known. I'd thought I'd seen it all—the fear, the sadness, even despair—but all that, I suddenly realised, had been mere scar tissue. In his final moments, they parted like flaps of dead flesh and I saw the real him, red and raw.

I jumped as the windows slammed shut with a bang. Even through the closed windows I could hear the howling outside growing louder, more insistent. Something was coming. Something evil.

"I see it!" he screamed. "Oh my god, I see it." His eyes were staring straight ahead, and I was certain that it wasn't anything of this world that he was seeing. The lights seemed to wither in the presence of something overwhelming in the room, like we were in the shadow of some immense bird of prey circling overhead. With a yell I let go of his arm, my fingertips stinging—red, almost burnt. He was quiet, and he no longer moved. His jaw hung slightly open, a tenuous thread of drool reaching for his chin. Terror-stricken, I looked on as the life in his eyes dwindled—then petered out like a smoking cinder.

The wind had died down. It seemed to me the room grew a little brighter, showing all the more clearly, in its light, the pale and lifeless shell lying next to me on the couch, and I knew that it was over. When I'd stopped shaking, I carefully I studied his chest for signs of breathing, and I slowly extended my hand to feel for a pulse, only to pull away at the last moment. I didn't need any trouble. There was nothing to be done. I thought about calling for an ambulance, but what the hell would I tell them?

I took one last look at Leon at the door. Then, reaching for the switch, I turned off the lights, and in less than a minute I was back in the car and driving into the deep of the night.

TAKEN FOR A RIDE

Her ears were still buzzing with the leftover pounding sounds of the club as she stumbled out into the surprising coolness of the night—or very early morning. But even the bracing outside air wasn't enough to purge the alcohol from her veins. The world around her stayed perfectly still—until she moved her head in the slightest, whereupon everything would sway and bob with nauseating fervour. A lamppost, glowing a lurid orange, spun madly above her head. *Wonder Woman gone wild with her Lasso of Truth*, her mind somehow managed to conjure, much to her own amusement. She giggled, then stopped short when she tasted bile at the back of her throat.

"Fuck!" She was now on her knees, her palms pressing hideously against the rough tarmac of the road. She retched but came up empty. The club toilet had already had the honours.

"My god, Vera!" She heard high heels clopping towards her somewhere from the left, then frantic hands pulling at her shoulders and hair.

"Imma okay," she mumbled weakly, more for her own benefit than anyone else's.

"I told you not to finish the whole jug by yourself, babe."

"My god, Tessie, you can be such a nag. Nag, nag, nag. You gotta stop doing that. It makes you such an auntie." She burst into laughter. "Tessie the auntie!" she yelled. Somehow, it seemed very important that everyone in the vicinity should know that fact.

"You're drunk," the auntie said shortly. She seemed pissed.

"No shit, Sherlock."

"Come on, we have to get you home."

She heard Tessie whispering urgently to someone else. A man—deep voice. Vincent. That dude had carried a torch for Tessie ever since he laid eyes on her in Year One. Not that he ever had a shot, no, no. He was a nerd—and a real one too: one of those who actually knew how computers worked. Any laptop problems the girls had, he took on without further question, and the laptops always came back working like a charm.

Vera hadn't wanted him to join them for clubbing though, but Tessie had somehow persuaded her that it would be okay. He drove, and more importantly, he didn't drink. Oh, what a sight it must have been, a gargoyle like him gyrating next to two lovely ladies. Ha ha, oh yes, a gargoyle—that was what he was.

"Vince, I know it's really out of the way, but do you think you could give Vera a lift home? She's really not in a state to be taking a cab."

Vera, now in an awkward and unglamorous crouch position, her elbows braced against the insides of her thighs as they splayed right open (thank god she was wearing jeans), kept her eyes closed as she tried to calm the screaming banshee floating somewhere between her ears. Even without looking, she could imagine it: Vincent obligingly saying yes, but unable to keep the disappointment from blossoming in his eyes. This had to be the highlight of the night for him, she knew. Having Tessie all to himself as he drove her back, perhaps imagining that this was a precursor of greater things to come.

That was when a shaft of generosity (and genius) hit her. You could pay people to drive you, couldn't you? Why should she get in the way of the two (potential) lovebirds?

"No, no, guys," she said, trying to keep her words from slurring. "I'm going to get a taxi. Nope—a Fetch." She felt immensely pleased with herself. Using a private-hire service like Fetch would undoubtedly save her quite a few bucks. And bucks were important nowadays. Money was tight, wasn't it? Yes, yes, money was tight.

"You have got to be kidding, Vera. Look at yourself." It was Tessie, being oh-so-stern. Like a mother, really. She could be really annoying that way.

"No, I'm fine, really," she insisted. How could she show them that she was fine? "Look, look at me. Can I do this if I'm dr—"

Strong arms caught her just before she hit the ground. "You—you shouldn't try to dance right now, Vera," Vincent said. "I can send you home. It's really no trouble at all."

She struggled madly to escape his clutches. He was really strong. Irritation pricked her, and she threw a few punches wildly. "Let me go!"

The iron grip remained.

She bared her teeth. "I'm gonna bite!"

"Fuck, Vera, chill. Vince, just let her go."

She nearly fell again as he released his hold.

"Vera…" Tessie began, but she already knew what she had to do to rid herself of the two worrywarts. She whipped out her phone, and acting on pure muscle memory (because, really, any higher brain function had long ceased to exist), her fingers tapped rapidly on the screen.

"There—done!" she cried triumphantly, holding her phone aloft like a trophy. "Your Fetch driver will be arriving in approximately five minutes."

"Just cancel it, dammit."

"*Tsk, tsk*," she admonished, wagging a finger. "Don't you know there's now a cancellation fee?"

"Oh, Vera—" Tessie's exasperated groan told her she had won. "Vera, Vera…" Her friend drew her close, her voice falling to a whisper. "What about the Fetch rapist-killer? Aren't you worried?"

A distant sense of unease stirred in her stomach. She'd forgotten all about it. The Fetch Strangler, as the internet called him, after his favoured manner of killing. He was still at large after two horrific assaults and murders, despite the best efforts of the police (and Fetch, according to Fetch). The ride-hailing company said that someone had compromised their database, masking the true identity of the victims' driver—all they could trace were a fake photograph, fake vehicle licence plate and fake identity number. Hacked—they'd been hacked. But the vulnerability had been discovered and patched, Fetch reassured the public. And since it had been three months since the last attack, people were starting to believe them. But the doubt—it never went away.

What was she to do? Heck, what were the odds? And plus, it would be embarrassing to change her mind now.

"Naaah," she said. "That monster has a type, remember? He seems to like girls who look like you." She laughed, but it seemed to ring hollow. It was true, though. The two victims (and Tessie) shared some striking physical similarities: long hair with reddish-brown highlights, tall and slim. Could be a coincidence, of course. But with a pixie cut, and barely scraping 1.5 metres, she had to be safe. She had to be. And really, out of the tens of thousands of drivers out there, what were the odds?

Her phone buzzed. *Your driver is almost here.* All right, some precautions wouldn't hurt. She tapped on the driver's photograph and zoomed in. Young, perhaps in his 30s. Certainly not the fatherly 50-something she was hoping for. She took a screenshot. "Look, I'll send the photo to you. And when I get on board, I'll study every inch of his face to make sure he's the one in the photo."

Her ride was here. A white Toyota Altis, as stated in the app. Common, nondescript. Something a murderer would drive, wasn't it? *Shut up*, she told her brain. Licence plate number—a match. The bracing night air, paired with the rush of adrenaline, had chipped much of her drunkenness away. The car seemed so innocuous, its engine purring patiently as it sat waiting for her. It had pulled up slightly ahead, such that they could only see the back of the driver— just his silhouette, really.

Well, it wasn't the time to be shy. She walked right up to the front of the car and peered through the windscreen. The driver was sneezing into a tissue, his face all but obscured. She waited, two seconds, five seconds, but still he continued. He noticed her and beckoned her to board. She hesitated, and again he waved her in, this time with a tinge of impatience. His other hand, still holding the tissue, never left his face.

All right, she couldn't just stand there and stare the whole night. Steeling herself, she nodded bravely at Tessie, opened the rear car door and got in.

The driver had stopped sneezing. "Hi," she said, trying to make out the driver's face in the rear view mirror. She saw only his eyes.

He said nothing. The car moved off, and she couldn't resist the urge to turn back to look at Tessie's fast-receding figure.

Let's hope it's not the last time I see you.

The inside of the car felt like a cage. She stole a glance at the back of the driver. Who was she locked in with—a decent human being or a dangerous predator? Taking a deep breath, she glanced outside. They were hurtling down the expressway, (hopefully) heading home.

She tried again. "Busy night for you?"

"Yeah." His voice was gravelly, as if he had a cold. "Friday nights busy."

"All the clubbing and partying, eh?"

A cold silence. Then: "You party a lot?"

"N-no. Just a bit." Her mind whirred as she grasped wildly for something to say. "How's it like being a Fetch driver? Do you like it?"

"What do you think?" There was an edge to his voice now. "People like you out partying, and I have to work all the way till morning. If it's you, you think you will like it?"

"N-no, no, sorry."

"You people have no idea lah. To you, people like us are invisible. All you care about is cheap, cheap, cheaper. If we don't earn enough, do you care? You only complain why Fetch no more promos. Why no more discounts."

She bit her lip. Better not to say anything.

"You don't know how lucky you are, seriously." His eyes, in the rearview mirror, lingered on her. "You are young, pretty, well-educated. You have a bright future ahead. Me, I'll be lucky if I can continue driving when I'm old and weak." His eyes were trained on her, unblinking. "*Tong ren bu tong ming.*" People have such different fates.

She leaned back into the seat, wishing it would swallow her up. She never knew how to respond to sentiments like that.

Yes, yes, thank goodness I'm luckier than you are.

No, no, we decide our own fates.

Either seemed liable to get her thrown out of the car. Or worse. She stared out of the window, hoping that he would soon tire of ranting.

A cold tingle of fear dribbled into her gut. "Er, mister, where are you going? This is the wrong way."

"You didn't say which way you wanted what. This way faster."

They were no longer on the expressway. The road outside was narrow and dimly lit, lined on both sides by what seemed like dark forest. *Shit, shit, shit!* She'd allowed herself to be distracted, and now she had no idea where he'd driven her to. She frantically dug into her handbag. Her phone's GPS would easily tell her if they were indeed on the way home. *Thank god for technology!*

Her fingers closed round the familiar shape and whipped it out. She caught sight of her own expression in the black screen—half-panicked, half-relieved. Then she watched her eyes widen in horror as the screen stayed black. She pressed the home button, power button, volume buttons. Still black.

Battery flat.

Fuck technology!

———

Tessie stared worriedly at her phone. "She said she'd send me the driver's photo."

"She's half-drunk. Probably forgot all about it." Vincent didn't look away from the road.

"Maybe." She stared out of the window. "I think I'll call her, just to be safe."

"Oh, come on, you're overthinking."

"It won't hurt." She pressed her phone to her ear. "Come on, Vera. Come on. Just pick up, dammit."

Vera collapsed back into the seat, defeated. If he heard her little cry of despair, he said nothing. Was he gloating in silence? Or merely inured to the little individual idiosyncrasies he must surely witness almost every day?

Her eyes watched the passing trees anxiously. Should she ask him to stop the car? If he was willing to, surely that must confirm his innocence. *Or*, wily murderer that he was, why not let her off? Where could she go anyway, alone and helpless in the middle of nowhere? He could even pretend to drive off and circle back again in a few minutes, and she would still be there. Play with his food a little.

I hate you, brain. Just shut up already.

She had to think. Every passing minute was quite possibly a minute nearer to a horrifying end. Her heart shuddered as she caught sight of his eyes watching her from the rearview mirror. *Act normal. Be cool.*

"Where are we now?"

"Mount Pleasant Road. We'll be turning out to Thomson Road soon." Smooth, no hesitation. Glib, almost, like he had rehearsed the line.

"Do you have a power bank I can borrow? My phone is dead."

To her surprise, he passed her a cable. "You can charge directly from the car."

She almost screamed in relief. There, if that didn't prove his innocence, she didn't what would. Waiting for her phone screen to come to life, she felt her heart beat slowing—until she realised that the car was slowing too.

"Why are you stopping here!" she half-shouted. Her eyes frantically scanned the outside of the car. They were still on the dark, narrow lane, and it seemed to go on forever. No main road in sight.

"Left side feels a bit weird. Making strange noises. I need to check." The car rolled to a stop, and with a loud slam of the door she was left alone in the car.

What—the—fuck! Alarm bells were going off now. She hadn't heard any noise, and the car had been moving just fine. It sounded like a page right out of a serial killer's playbook. Get the victim somewhere deserted, feign some sort of car trouble, stop the car.

But her phone! She could still use her phone. "C'mon, c'mon," she muttered. The screen stayed blank.

The silence finally penetrated her consciousness. The engine was no longer running. Her phone wouldn't charge like that. *This guy knows what he's doing*, she realised, her blood running cold. Everything so far had been immaculately executed.

The bitter rant to distract her while he deviated off course, then pretending to let her charge her phone to allay her suspicions, only to cut off power at the critical moment. *He's definitely done this before.*

She stared numbly at her dead phone. Two clear droplets plopped onto the screen, and her mind, faraway, vaguely marvelled: *I'm crying. I'm about to be murdered, and all I can do is cry like a little bitch.*

Fuck this. If she was going to die, she wasn't going down without a fight. Where was the bastard? She swung her head around wildly. He was nowhere to be seen. Was he lurking about somewhere among the trees, waiting for an opportune time to strike? Should she get out of the car? It might give her the element of surprise. Yes, yes, she was a sitting duck in here. At least outside she could try to make a dash for it.

All right, all right, this is it. She braced herself as she reached for the door latch. Her heart was beating so furiously that her face felt as if it might explode. She paused. She reached downwards, unstrapped her heels with a few deft movements and kicked them off. There, now she was ready.

She scanned the outside again. Nothing.

Okay, it was now or never.

She flung the door open. Heart nearly bursting, she winced as she felt the rough tarmac slam against her bare feet. *Go, go, go!*

She ran. She ran like she'd never run before. Her thighs burned, her calves burned, her feet burned. Her eyes scoured the horizon desperately. *Please, please, please. Where's the main road!*

She heard a shout behind her, then running footfalls, startling near. "Miss! Miss! Why are you running?"

She didn't dare turn around. *Faster!* she urged her legs. But they only screamed in response. Her lungs joined the chorus.

Then she heard it. The faint roar of traffic. Squinting her eyes, she thought she could see cars whipping across the small gap in the trees far, far ahead. *Yes!*

"Miss, please, come back!" He seemed even closer now.

Air was precious, air was in short supply, but she thought it worthwhile to suck in a few extra mouthfuls just to shout: "Fuck off, bastard!"

It was a mistake. The exertion threw her slightly off balance, and her steps began to falter. Every stride grew more erratic, less sure, till at last she was diving headlong into the dark sea of the road. There was an almighty crack as her chin connected with the surface, and the shockwaves seemed to reverberate through her skull. With her last bit of strength, before her world turned black, she painfully turned herself over with her elbows. She heard panting, the brutal scraping of shoes on road. Then, he loomed over her, grin on face.

"Where you running off to, miss?"

———

"Please, Vince. She's not picking up."

"She'll be fine, Tessie. You know what she's like. She always turns up okay."

"Please, just swing by her place before you drop me off. I know it's out of the way but it would mean so, so much to me. Please, Vince?"

There was a sharp intake of breath. Eyes still ahead, he spoke slowly. "What I don't understand, Tessie, is why you give a shit about her at all. Look at how she treats you, how she speaks to—"

"She was just drunk, Vince. You know she's always running her mouth off. But she—"

"That's exactly what I mean! You're always defending her, sticking up for her. Does this bitch deserve this sort of loyalty from you?"

She felt an icy anger rise from within. He was forgetting his place. "She's my friend."

"And what about those who truly care about you, Tessie? What about them?"

"You mean, like *you*?" She didn't even try to keep the sneer out of her voice.

"Like me," he said softly. "Like me."

She laughed. A small, mocking laugh. "You want to know what you are to me? You really do?"

His lips trembled. He licked them quickly, nervously, as if comforting himself. All the while, he said nothing.

"Just *drive*, Vincent," she said, spitting out the words. "If you won't fetch me to Vera's place, just tell me, and I'll take a taxi."

He gave a small, steely nod. With a sharp lurch and a squeal from the tires, the car rolled and veered left, exiting the expressway.

—⁓—

Her head was on fire. Or at least it felt like it. She gingerly reached for her chin, and her fingers came back wet and warm.

It all came back to her in a jolt.

She sprang to her feet. Tried to, at least. Strong arms caught her by the shoulders as she wavered and fell. Instinctively, she scratched and clawed. "Don't touch me!" she screamed.

The vice-like grip did not yield. "Calm down, lady! What the hell is wrong with you?"

Her eyes swivelled around frenziedly. They were back at the car. He must have carried her back while she'd been out cold. She felt her strength and courage drain.

"Please, please," she began to whimper. "Don't hurt me, please. Just let me go. I won't tell a soul what happened."

He released her so abruptly that she promptly collapsed onto the floor in a heap. "I'm not going to hurt you," he blurted out, his eyes now worried.

Her eyes shot up in surprise. Something in his voice made her believe him. "Y-you're not?"

"Of course not. Just what the hell are you thinking, miss?"

"But—you just—you just stopped—in the middle of nowhere—"

He sighed. "Come here," he said, moving over to the other side of the vehicle.

She scrambled to her feet and followed him.

"You see that, miss?"

She stared, not quite believing her eyes. Then, as it sank in, she began to laugh. She laughed and laughed.

The driver folded his arms and stared at his passenger anxiously, wondering if he'd picked up a lunatic. First, the senseless screaming and scratching, and now this. He'd never seen anyone laugh at a flat tire so heartily before.

"You sure, babe? You sure you're okay? All right, then."

Tessie settled back with a sigh of relief. Turning to Vincent, she said, "That was Vera. She's fine. You can turn back now."

"Okay." He seemed tense, on edge.

She turned away. The sight of him was starting to irk her.

"Where are we?" she said sharply, peering outside. "This doesn't look like the way to Vera's place."

"Tessie."

"What?"

"You know, don't you?"

"Know what?"

The car slowed to a stop. She stared worriedly through the car window. There didn't seem to be any traffic on the road at all. She turned to him, voice softening. "Vince, you're scaring me."

He unbuckled his seat belt and turned to her. "Tessie, you must know how much I care about you. You *must*."

"Vince, just drive, please. Vince—"

"I tried, you know, with the others. Tried to pretend they were you. But it's no use, Tessie. All I can think of is you."

She opened her mouth to scream, but all she could manage was a small choking sound as strong hands closed around her throat. The last sound she heard, as she stared up helplessly into the eyes of a stranger, were words in a gruff, shaky voice, almost in tears.

"I love you, Tessie."

LINES

He had never been much of a writer, but he supposed a suicide note was about as good as any place to start. Logically speaking, there was really no reason to leave a note, much less fret over its contents, but he couldn't—no, he certainly could not—leave everyone behind without telling why. It was love, he supposed, love. The love for his children, the one good thing that had come of his marriage. The love, even—dare he say it?—for his wife, but very likely not the kind of love she was looking for. And yes, inconceivable as it was, the love for his parents, who had made his life living hell from the time he was twelve.

Love, damn it all.

And if he were to be honest with himself, also just the slightest dash of vindictiveness. *See what you've done. See what you've made me do.* The final finger in their faces to remind them that it was he who had the last laugh, he who refused to live life on *their* terms.

Now, all he had to do was gather all that feeling, all that love and hate and everything in between, and turn all of it to words on paper. No sweat. Ha.

He could feel the familiar sinking feeling. Staring at an assignment, knowing how important it was, and not being able to write down a single word. It was like school all over again.

Relax, he told himself, *there's plenty of time*. Margaret was away on a business trip, due to return only the next morning. Dan and Elaine were away at their respective school camps, back only the day after. Margaret would be the one to find him, as was appropriate. And it would be a peaceful farewell, too, for both his and her sake; no flinging himself from the top-most floor of their condominium, but the gentle going-away his stash of strong sleeping pills would provide. He had everything planned out. He just didn't know the words with which to say adieu.

Without realising it, he had drifted off to the balcony, where the patter and petrichor of a gentle drizzle brought him back to another time.

———ᴧᴧᴧ———

They sat on a bench, a respectable distance between them, staring out at the park being drenched by the downpour.

Daniel had to shout to be heard.

"Is it better to be an asymptote, coming infinitely close but never touching the axis, or to be one of two intersecting lines, meeting once and never again?"

Gregory laughed. "What sort of stupid question is that?"

The other man stared dreamily into the rain. "The kind Math teachers spend their time thinking about, my dear."

Gregory stiffened. He hissed. "I told you never to call me that."

"Not even when we're alone?"

"You never know who might be listening."

Daniel sighed. "No one's going to hear us above the rain, Greg," he said gently. He hesitated for a moment, then continued: "Anyone would think you're ashamed of me."

"Stop saying that." Gregory's face was burning—whether from embarrassment or anger, he didn't know. "You know we both could lose our jobs. Nobody wants someone like us teaching kids."

"All right. I'm sorry."

Gregory looked at the person he loved more than anyone in the world, and he felt a pang in his heart. He ripped his hand from where it'd been stuck fast to his hip, letting it fall against the cold stone of the bench. It searched, seeking warmth, companionship...and found the hand that was already waiting, that had always been waiting.

—〰—

Gregory was shaken from his reverie by the wetness on his cheeks. The rain, swept in by the wind, or he'd been crying again. Twenty years. Surely that ought to be long enough for the past to die, but some memories had a way of returning from the dead. Not that he would have it any other way, though. He felt himself reaching for the ring that he wore around his neck. A memento from a dear friend, he had always told his wife. That much was true.

Just touch it and think of me, and I'll be there. That had been Daniel's promise.

Where are you, Danny? he wondered, staring into the rain.

—〰—

Danny was dead. And it was all his fault. Why had he insisted on breaking up, even though Danny begged and begged him not to?

But what choice did he have? He'd been called to the principal's office the week before, and did he not try his damnedest to fight back?

He remembered the superior nose, the nasal voice. "There are some lines that can't be crossed, Gregory. This is one of them."

"With all due respect, sir, I don't see it in the Ministry's directives."

The principal leaned in close, so close that it was possible to see the short hairs of his moustache rattling like tiny sabres in the draught from his nose.

"It's not in there. It's an invisible line, but it's a line as real and solid as any other." The principal's expression softened, slightly. "Gregory, you're a good teacher. The students like you. So please, don't do this. Don't carry on like this."

"Carry on like this?"

"You know what I mean. This perverse... engagement. Someone saw you holding hands, Gregory. *Holding hands!*" The principal's face was red. Then, in almost a whisper, thick with horror and scandal: "*With another man.*"

He didn't know where he found his voice. "I have the right to love too, you know."

The principal glared at him. "Of course you do. A woman, any woman you choose. Tall, short, ugly, beautiful—god, there are millions of them out there, go choose *any* one of them, for goodness' sake.

"Or if you cannot, leave. Leave the service. Think of the children, Gregory, think of them. How can you have them following your example?"

Those damned beady eyes, the same eyes that allowed themselves to dwell on the pretty young teachers, who averted their gazes nervously. The thin, cruel lips that insisted that no female teacher wear pants while in school—most unbecoming of a lady, he said—while making the most sordid of remarks as the eyes took in, approvingly or otherwise, the contours of their legs.

But he was powerless. He wasn't simply facing up to the tyranny of a single man—no, he knew the entire weight of the Ministry was behind the despot. It was going to be him against everyone else—the rest of the school, the rest of society. There was no fighting this Goliath.

Danny didn't take it well. In a mad whirlwind of tempestuous rage and despair, he took his own life, leaving Gregory well and truly alone in the world.

And he had been alone ever since.

—⁓—

A cold wind brought him back. With a start, he realised he wasn't alone.

"Intersecting lines, Greg," he heard a voice behind him say. A voice that, despite the intervening years, hadn't lost any of its familiarity.

"Danny?" He couldn't bring himself to turn around.

"Yes."

The initial chill he had felt evaporated. A warm longing filled his heart, and with it a painful twinge. "I'm so sorry, Danny. I let you down. I, I…"

He felt a warm hand on his. "There's nothing to apologise for. You did what you had to do."

Tears filled his eyes. He turned—a faint frisson passed through him, then evaporated. Danny looked the same. Those wide, innocent eyes and those pale, sensitive lips that turned with every wave of emotion that crossed his heart. He didn't look a day older than the day he died—but he looked different, somehow. Maybe death did that to a person.

"Why are you here?" he asked as his hand reached for the face he loved the most. "Why haven't you...moved on?" Danny's lips broke into a sad smile. There it was again—something harder, almost cruel, creeping into the once-soft features. He felt his heart beat a little faster as a question began burning on his lips. "Are you—are you here for vengeance?"

There was surprise, which bloomed into laughter. The hearty, unrestrained laughter of old. He felt warm arms embrace him. "Vengeance doesn't keep someone around for decades, Greg," he heard Danny whisper in his ear. "Only love does." Danny took a step back and gazed into his eyes. "Don't do it, my dear. There's still so much to live for."

"Is there? Stuck in a loveless marriage. Never ever being able to be the person I am."

"Not loveless. She knows, Greg. She knows, and she accepts you for who you are. You should, too."

"But what am I supposed to *do*?" He heard a familiar note of despair ringing in his own voice. "I have children, children I love. I can't just leave."

"It won't be easy, no, but it can be figured out. Killing yourself isn't the answer. Trust me, I ought to know." A short, wry laugh. "But listen to me"—Danny's voice grew firm, urgent—"don't let yourself hate, okay? Don't hate the world for what it's done to you, to us. They've already taken so much of our humanity. Don't let them take even more."

Danny turned to go, but was stayed by Gregory's hand. "Something happened, didn't it? Tell me, Dan. Tell me."

There was hesitation, but eventually his lover spoke. "Hate, Greg, hate happened. A long, time ago."

"What happened?" he insisted.

The reply came slowly. "Someone died."

He felt a faint stirring in the back of his mind, the murmuring and rousing of ancient, time-encrusted memories. *Someone died.* He had a feeling he knew who. "Charles. Principal Charles."

He saw the same glint in his lover's eye, that of cold steel—then a deep, abiding sadness.

Principal Charles had died a few months after Danny took his own life. A car accident, they were all told, most unfortunate and unexpected. Driving alone late at night, he had suddenly swerved off the road and into a tree, dying before the ambulance could arrive. No one asked why he had swerved...

"You were there, weren't you, Danny?"

"I didn't mean for it to happen...I think," Danny said very softly. "I don't know. I just wanted to confront him, wanted him to answer for what he did. But when he saw me, he panicked. He panicked, Greg, and he died because of me. I thought I would be happy, but I wasn't. For all the time I've roamed this Earth after my death, I've never known peace." Danny stared at him, his eyes a mix of longing and sorrow. "Until now."

"Don't go, please," Gregory heard himself saying. "Don't leave me alone." His hand reached forward, but found nothing.

"I have to go, my dear. But you aren't alone. You won't ever have to be alone."

"Will I see you again? When everything is over."

"I don't know, Greg, I don't know. But I know this—it is better to have loved and lost, than never to have loved at all. Intersecting lines, that's what we are. Whatever it is, whatever it'll be, I just want you to know that you'll always be loved."

—✺—

For a long time after Danny left, Gregory stared absently ahead. Then, like a man waking from a dream, he rose at last, a wistful smile on his lips. Hands gripping the railing, he looked intently into the fading rain and, for just a fleeting moment, thought he saw the faint promise of a rainbow in the distance.

THE BLAZE

I awake to every pore screaming in agony. My limbs are stiff, unresponsive slabs of meat that lie uselessly around me. I can feel them twitching in response, I think, to some vestigial impulse my brain flung out hours or days ago. I cry out—or try to—but the cloth muffling my mouth won't let me be heard. Exhausted by these meagre efforts, I fall back into a pain-hazed slumber.

When I next open my eyes, a figure in white stares down at me.

"You're awake," she says matter-of-factly, giving me a faint smile. "How are you feeling?"

"Terrible," I croak, wondering if she can make out the words pushing futilely against the gag. "What happened to me?"

Either she didn't hear me, or she didn't want to answer. She turns and leaves the room, and I'm all alone in a thick and blistering silence.

—◠◠◠—

They are screaming. Dancing and shrieking, their heads of orange aglow. A sea of people, bobbing grotesquely to some hideous beat that eludes my ears. My god, did they have to scream so loud? On fire, they—we—we are all on fire. Giant matchsticks lit on fire, twitching, jiggling in agony, charred black heads adorned by viciously crackling flames.

———∿∿∿———

I wake up screaming.

Someone is at my ear, whispering, soothing me. She straightens up and takes a few steps back. "I'm going to increase your dosage of morphine. It'll make you feel better."

She sounds sincere, but I don't believe her. Nothing can take away the pain, the heat. My stomach is a great big roaring fire and the fat under my skin sizzles and simmers and smokes. The heat, my god, the kind of heat that fills your head with a throbbing buzz and your nostrils with the stench of superheated metal. *I'm going to scream. I'm going to scream and scream and scream because nobody knows I'm burning up inside and nobody can take away the pain. The furnace, the heat...*

My thoughts slow and slur. Distantly I remember something I've read before: when your nerve endings have been scorched to a cinder, you feel no more pain. That, I decide, is what is happening to me. The gentle cool of relief washes over me. It is over. It is going to be over very soon.

—∿∿—

Much later, it seems, there are voices.

"I'm not sure he's fully lucid, but you can try. But please, don't agitate him. He isn't in a very stable condition." A woman's voice.

A reassuring voice answers. This voice, it's deeper and has a more authoritative ring to it. It lets you know it is in charge, but not so that you mind. *Leave it to me*, it seems to say. *Leave it to me, and it'll all be fine.*

"Mr Choy, can you hear me?" the voice asks.

"Y-yes." I don't know how the words get out of my parched mouth, but they sound almost like me. Almost.

"It's all right, sir. Take it easy." He speaks slowly, clearly. Like to a child. "I'll just ask you a few questions, and if you can, only if you can, you just tell me what you know, okay?"

The figure is coming into view. Blurry at first, a blurry blue. Shiny buttons. Very shiny. They catch the light and glitter like silver ingots.

"Can you remember what happened, sir?"

Happened. What happened. The unholy glow, the searing heat, the screaming. Oh, the screaming.

"Fi-i-ire." A simple word, and it takes forever to get it out of my throat. Excess saliva gurgles at the back of my throat. My questioner has to see it. The pain I'm in. The smell. The smell of cooking flesh, rising from beneath the bandages they have plastered all over me.

"Yes, Mr Choy, a fire. You were caught in it. Can you remember how it started?"

Start? It didn't start. It just came, washing over us like a wave of searing heat. The pain—does he understand the pain?

"F-fire."

"It's the morphine, I think." The feminine voice is back. "Or he's delirious. Or both. I think you should come back later."

"Sure."

And there's silence once again.

———

I dream of her, beautiful, soft. The coolness of her touch, her skin on mine.

"Hush," I tell her, "don't scream anymore."

"I'm not, darling." She's smiling radiantly, a blinding light behind her hair. Blindingly white, then yellow, then a ghastly orange.

She starts screaming.

The figure in white is back.

"Hi, Mr Choy. I'm Doctor Koh. Hope you're feeling better."

"It hurts so much. What happened?" I'm vaguely aware that I've been meaning to ask something else, but now that she's here it eludes me.

"A nasty accident, I'm afraid. But luckily the worst is behind you." She smiles down at me kindly, then turns to the machines beside me.

"What accident?" My god, the screaming, the burning. I wasn't just dreaming. It happened. "Doctor," I plead, reaching for her arm, "tell me what happened." A mistake—I can almost hear something ripping beneath the bandages, and I stifle a cry of pain.

Her smile disappears. "Please, calm down." A gentle but firm hand on my shoulder. "Lie back, rest some more. The police will be here in a bit. They can tell you what happened exactly. They have all the details."

I lie back, but rest is the last thing on my mind. Something…something is floating just below the surface of my consciousness, bobbing, almost showing—Damn! I nearly had it.

The police officer arrives just as I am about to doze off, but the drowsiness falls away when I see the figure in blue. But, wary of worsening the damage, I will myself to be still. I focus everything into my voice: "Officer, tell me what happened. I need to know, please."

The officer is a solemn, fresh-faced young man. He may be new to the job, a national serviceman even, but if so he doesn't show it one bit.

"You were at a hotpot restaurant, sir," he says, without missing a beat. "Witnesses say there was a loud bang and an explosion, and we suspect the gas tank is to blame. That's all we know for now."

And just like that, the question I've been meaning to ask comes to me.

"Where's Mandy?" I almost yell. "My girlfriend, is she okay?"

He regards me sternly for a moment, before retrieving a notebook from his breast pocket. He flips through the pages methodically, his eyes scanning through the contents without the slightest flicker of emotion, and all this while I try to lie as still as possible, biting down on the panic that threatens to overwhelm me.

"Sir," he finally says in a most severe tone, "you were with two other male friends. They are unharmed, if that is your question. They were at the toilet when the explosion occurred."

"My girlfriend, my girlfriend," I insist, beginning to wheeze. Out of the corner of my eye I can see that the good doctor is at the doorway, about to intervene. "Please—my girlfriend!"

"There wasn't any woman with you, sir. Your friends confirmed it was j—"

"I'm very sorry, officer, but you have to leave. Right now." The doctor is by my side, drawing out some liquid from a vial with a syringe. "Right *now*."

I close my eyes, allowing the sedative's warm wave to take me.

—⁓—

"You mustn't agitate yourself like that," she says sternly, when I awake from my dreamless sleep. Her face softens. "We nearly lost you when you first came in, you know? You have to take it easy."

"What do you mean?" I ask weakly, uninterested. My head is groggy, and it is beginning to hurt everywhere again.

She is on the verge of speech, but she hesitates. Bits and pieces of what happened are beginning to stream back into my head: the police officer, the explosion—Mandy.

This time there isn't any surge of panic, just a deep unease. "Doctor, do you know what happened to Mandy? My girlfriend."

She bites her lip. "Your friends came over just now, while you were unconscious. Seeing that you were so anxious to know what happened to your girlfriend, I thought I would ask them, in case they weren't around when you awoke. Hope you don't mind."

"Not at all. Just tell me, please."

She gives a small sigh and pulls up a chair to my side. She sits and leans forward, her fingers interlaced, as if in a gesture of prayer.

"There's no easy way to tell you this, so I'm just going to go straight to it. Your girlfriend died months ago, during a diving expedition. She drowned."

"That can't be right." I shake my head stubbornly. "I saw her. I saw the others. They were burning, crying, screaming."

"Mr Choy," she says sternly, looking me in the eye, "there was no one else caught in the explosion. Just you. No, I said"—as I try to sit up to protest—"just you. No one else."

"Impossible," I mumble. "I saw…"

"You've been through a lot of trauma, Mr Choy. Sometimes, in situations like this, the brain makes things up, things that didn't happen. Whatever you dreamt, or thought you saw, it wasn't real. It didn't happen."

A thought strikes me. "You said something about almost losing me when I came in. What's that about?"

"Oh, that. When you first came to us at the ER, there was a moment your heart wasn't beating. You

were dead, clinically speaking, for a minute or two."
She looks down at me with a most maternal smile,
even though she's probably no older than I am. "We
pulled you back from the brink."

Back from the dead.

"You know," she says, still smiling, "I've had
patients like you who later claimed that they'd
caught a glimpse of the afterlife. You didn't see
anything...?" She trails off abruptly, growing pale.
"No, no, I'm sorry. I shouldn't be encouraging this
sort of thinking."

It hits me just a moment later. What I witnessed:
the fire, the burning...it was hellfire. It was real after
all. It wasn't the mad gibbering of a mind reeling
from trauma. I saw it—experienced it—for just a
moment when I was dead.

"Oh, my god."

"Mr Choy, you mustn't let your imagination run
wild. Please."

Mandy was screaming. She was burning. Oh god.
They were all screaming and burning. And so was I...

"Mr Choy!"

My vision is blurring. A distant female voice is
shouting. *"Code 10. Code 10. I need help in here,
stat! Patient is going into cardiac arrest."*

I feel my body getting hot. The light, it's blinding.
My nose is full of the stench of sulphur and suffering.
The terrible grinding and gnashing of teeth around

me grows louder and louder—oh, the wails! The wails of the damned!

"We're losing him—I'm starting CPR!"

I want to beg, to plead, but already I can feel the flesh melting off my lips.

SWAN SONG

He hadn't changed much, not really. Still the same boyish face, now with deep grooves extending from the eyes, bearing testimony to his proclivity for smiling. He sure had much to smile about—he was one of the best oncologists in the country, and his practice had flourished to the point where he had an entire chain of clinics running under his banner. I knew this going in, and good thing too, because not once during our secondary school class reunion did he talk about his work.

"So, what's it like, knowing you can retire anytime you like?" I said, when I met Ajit at the gents. I was seeking a reprieve from Don's unremitting recitation of his recent successes at the dinner table, all amidst a sea of bored faces wishing he would shut up—that guy hadn't changed one bit either.

"It's no different, really. I can't see myself retiring anytime soon, anyway. Too much going on." He smiled, one of those I-wish-I-had-a-choice smiles that he had worn since he was a student.

"Sell it. Pass it on to a successor. You can do anything you like."

"Ah, if only it were that easy."

It was my turn to smile. "You always had a tough time abdicating your responsibilities."

"They are called responsibilities for a reason."

We laughed and hurried out of there as we heard Don's booming voice echoing down the corridor, towards us.

"He's been trying to corner me since the start of this evening," Ajit whispered, a rare spark of irritation flaring in his eyes.

"He wants to know how he's doing compared to you." I grinned. "He *has* to find out how you're doing now."

He rolled his eyes. "He's a lawyer. I'm a doctor. It's hardly apples to apples."

"Oh, trust me. He'll find a way."

His pace slowed, and his face settled into a strange sombreness. "It's like we're back in school all over again. Comparing report cards, vying for first place."

"Well, you'd been first in class for as long as I can remember. And he had always been a close second. I imagine it can't be nice always being the bridesmaid, never the bride. Perhaps he's hoping that things would be different now that we're adults."

He shook his head, and the lines on his face reappeared as a sad smile deepened on his face. "I wish things could be different too."

Two months later Ajit called me out of the blue.

"I have cancer," he said, his voice calm. Or devoid of emotion. It was hard to tell over the phone. The illness was very likely terminal, he said. He could hope to have a year at best.

I managed to get some poorly formed condolences out of my mouth. We were barely 45, and I, for one, thought we still had plenty of time.

"What will you do?" I asked at last, unable to stand the silence.

His answer was almost immediate. "Live."

He invited me over to his house on Sixth Avenue one weekend evening. I had expected a big house crowded with friends and family, but all that met me was a big house. My host, in contrast, cut a diminished figure in the dark doorway. I wondered if the cancer was already making its effect felt.

"I'm sorry," he said, looking sheepish. "There's no one else I could have asked. Hope you don't mind."

"No problem at all," I said, as I was led into a cavernous living room. It seemed an awful lot of space for just one person. "You and Anne...?" I said hesitantly.

"Divorced years ago. Guess that didn't come up during the reunion, eh?" A humourless laugh. "She never liked that I always put work first. Good thing we didn't have any children."

"Your mum doesn't live with you?"

"She did. She passed away a few years ago."

As we swirled the fine vintage he'd unbottled for my benefit, we talked. Or rather, he talked, in a desultory manner that can often serve as a prelude to more serious conversation as the night draws on. I mostly listened, and while I was at it, I slowly took in my surroundings. The décor was tastefully done, but there was such an overt note of professionalism that it was immediately clear my friend had no part in it, save for the paying. Not a single chair, couch or table out of place, or at odds with the general colour scheme. It was as if he had carved out an entire showroom from an interior design gallery and transplanted it here whole. My eyes searched for a personal touch, however awkward, however incongruous—some odd souvenir he'd picked up on one of his exotic holidays abroad, perhaps, or some knick-knack he'd once bought and since regretted, but exhibited all the same in an all-too-human display of sunk-cost fallacy. But I looked in vain. There was nothing, not even a photo.

On my first scan of the room I very nearly missed the grand piano hiding underneath a dust cover, probably a Steinway or something just as expensive. It was then I remembered—Ajit was a masterful musician. In fact—and here I decided to chip in on the conversation—wasn't it he who was offered a scholarship to read music at the Yong Siew Toh Conservatory of Music?

He nodded, and I thought I spotted a faint gleam of pride in his eyes.

"But you went to med school instead."

"I did. Had to be realistic."

"Do you still play?"

"Not the piano." He paused, and an air of uncertainty seemed to come over him. "I—There's something I want to show you."

He left the room. I wandered around, still looking for any article in the room that would tell me a little more about a friend I hadn't met for at least (not counting the reunion, of course) a good five or six years. And not for lack of trying too—he was just too busy, always. When I last visited his place, he was still living in his flat in Yishun, the one he'd gotten together with his then-wife. That had to be more than a decade back, I realised. He had come really far.

I was just about to give up on my search when my eyes fell upon a photo displayed in a frame lost in a forest of tall vases, in a distant corner of the room. It was Ajit and his mother, back when he had been, say, six or seven? His young, round face was radiant, showing all his teeth in a full-blown laugh. Holding his small hand was a woman in her mid-thirties, known to me as Auntie Reya. She looked the same as I remembered—the determined jaw, the eyes that could flash sternness and good humour in a single twinkle.

"I had no idea I still had that photo."

I turned around to see Ajit peering, almost curiously, at the frame I held in my hand. His own hands were on a enormous cello case that nearly reached his chin, which was now quivering slightly from the exertion of hauling the instrument over. I took the case from him, finding, to my surprise, that it was far lighter than it had looked in his hands.

"Thanks," he said, slightly breathless. "I got this on one of my trips to Europe some years back, but I only got to playing it after the diagnosis. It cost me a bomb."

With my help, and in small, painstaking motions, he set the whole thing up, then sank heavily into a chair as I held the instrument upright. Gently lowering the cello's neck into his waiting embrace, I could sense a palpable change come over him. His dull eyes came alive, and his frail body was seized by a current of energy I hadn't thought he would be able to muster. His fingers seemed to teem with some unseen electricity—when free, they appeared to twitch infinitesimally, but the moment they found the bow and instrument they became sure and supple. It was a marvellous transformation.

Then he played.

Oh, how he played. Our mundane surroundings dropped away, faded into nothing. The fingers on his left hand darted here and there with a virtuosity that was tremendous to behold, and his right guided the soulful crooning of the strings. What a song! I'd never heard it before in all my life, but there was a haunting familiarity about it—and beneath that lustrous melody, I was sure, a terrible and awful presence that allowed itself to be glimpsed every now and then. It was both frightening and irresistible, and I found myself halfway between relieved and frustrated when the music finally stopped.

"Just—just what song is that?" I said breathlessly, realising that I'd been holding my breath in.

"Oh, nothing in particular. I was just noodling around." He laid down the bow gently. "Quite a sound, eh?"

"Very impressive."

"It has a long history, apparently. The seller told me it came from Austria, if I'm not mistaken. It has a name too, in German or something. 'Giver of Life', or 'Life-giver', something fancy like that. I wasn't paying particular attention at the time, but now I wish I was." He looked down at the instrument lovingly. In the soft light of the room, the reddish-brown sheen of the lacquered wood almost glowed. With a sigh, he said, "If only I'd started playing it earlier. Think of all the lovely music I'd missed out on!"

"Better late than never," I said, smiling.

But something about the music bothered me, and I soon bid my host goodbye. That night, as I slept, I had the most peculiar dream. The contents of it eluded me the moment my eyes opened, but it left me with a lingering sense of dread the whole day after.

—〰—

A week later I was once again at the front door of my friend's house, but this time with a guest in tow. There was a buzzing excitement in my chest, but when the door opened and I caught sight of Ajit's pale, gaunt face, the feeling fizzled. He looked thinner, weaker than before. At the rate he was going, I thought worriedly, he wasn't going to make it a month, much less a year.

He must have seen the look on my face, for he smiled widely and clapped me on the shoulder.

"Don't look so glum, friend. I may look terrible, but I feel just fine. Who's your friend?"

I introduced Mark Schmidt, a friend from Germany who had most serendipitously stopped by Singapore for a musical festival. He was a musical conductor at a school, but even more importantly, he took a special interest in antique instruments.

Mark gave a small gasp as soon as he walked into the living room, where the cello was already resting on a stand beside a chair. "May I?" he asked, turning his gaze to his host for just the barest of moments before it snapped back to the dark and silent instrument.

Ajit smiled and nodded. Without wasting a second, Mark scrambled across the room and knelt by the cello, running his fingers almost reverently across the glossy wood. He muttered and exclaimed softly under his breath, his entire being heaving with great emotion.

After hearing the fifth "mein gott" emanating from the enthralled conductor, I sat down with Ajit on the couch and, grinning, said, "You have to give him a minute or two, I suppose. You won't be able to get a word out of him right now."

At length, my German friend rose to his feet and turned towards us, his face solemn. "Tell me, my friend," he said heavily, addressing Ajit, "where did you find this cello?"

His smile fast fading, Ajit told him about the antique store he'd come across while vacationing in Salzberg. "Is everything okay? It's not stolen or something, is it? I paid nearly twenty thousand euros for that."

"It's not stolen."

"Then what's wrong with it?"

"It has a history. Many people think it's cursed."

For a stunned moment Ajit and I exchanged bewildered glances. "But they told me it's called 'Life-giver'," he said softly.

" 'Life-giver'? Either they have the translation all wrong, or they're liars. This—this does not give life. It *takes* life."

As Ajit stared, mouth slightly agape, at the instrument of death, his hand unconsciously found its way to his hollow cheek. So he had noticed it too, how he was wasting away far more quickly than he was supposed to. He stared and stared, but I noticed his look was not one of horror, but contemplation.

Mark, embarrassed that he'd inadvertently been the bearer of such bad news, hurriedly added, without conviction: "But it's all legend, of course. You know what these antiques are like, full of blood and death and everything. If it has a good story, its value goes up, naturally."

But Ajit wasn't listening. There was a distant look in his eyes, and he was mouthing something I couldn't hear. Finally, he straightened up and smiled. "Gentlemen," he said, as if nothing in the past ten minutes had happened, "if you'd be so good as to hear me play a little tune."

With the air of a performer, he strode over to the cello. He seated himself, then lifted the instrument from the stand—again, with great effort—and set it down gently on its endpin. Slowly, deliberately, he laid the bow upon the waiting strings.

He played.

It was a song of longing, wistful and sorrowful, reaching straight for the heart. And as he played, he unravelled. I don't quite know how, but I *saw*. I saw Ajit, as a boy no more than 10 years old, staring tearfully out of the window as his friends whooped and yelled all the way to the playground. Auntie Reya was shouting in the background, telling him to get back to his books. Ajit, now a young adult, pleading with his mother as she flung his violin to the ground and stomped it to pieces. I heard words, some clear, some indistinct; I heard "duty as a son" and "responsibility to do your best". I saw him slogging away day and night, in the library, in the lab, and felt the resentment building up within. And then all at once all that was swept away and narrow confines gave way to vast vistas, infinite and boundless, and my heart shuddered and shook with inexplicable joy and longing.

And then all I saw was Ajit, as he was, playing. I saw his fingers moving furiously across the strings, as if making up for lost time, his bow making deep, incisive cuts, allowing more of himself to pour out. Was it his blood that was his music, or the other way round? I couldn't tell. His brow was furrowed with an intense concentration, but even with his head canted down, I could see that he was smiling.

Mark was stirring beside me, as if breaking out of the spell. He made to rise, but my hand was on him before he could do so. He looked at me, and I shook my head. He opened his mouth to protest, but at that moment the melody took such a heart-rending turn that he was quite overcome, and he dropped back to his seat like a sack of stones.

A visible change was unfolding over Ajit. His face seemed to lose substance even as he played, the hollow of his cheeks deepening with every plangent chord he struck. The sick feeling in my stomach grew, and I would have gotten up at that moment if I hadn't seen the tears glistening down the musician's cheeks in rapturous streams. If I were to be honest, I felt a burning awe—perhaps even envy.

Eventually the music drew to an end; the last note hanging in the air whimpered and died, and we were left in a roomful of silence. Ajit sat where he was, chin down, his chest lifting and sagging in rather feeble fits and starts.

"Come," I said at last, "you need to rest."

Ajit meekly allowed Mark and I to help him up and to his room. After we had settled him into bed, Ajit, opening his eyes, grasped my hand and smiled.

"Thank you, my friend. Thank you."

"What for?"

"For bearing witness to my music. I know it cannot have been easy for you." He gave a sigh and closed his eyes—for the last time, something in me suspected. Tears peeked out of the corners of his eyes. "Do you...do you know what it's like, never having your music heard?"

We left after we watched the sick man fall asleep. In complete silence, we coursed through the long, lonely corridors and exited the empty house.

Once outside, Mark came to life.

"Why on earth did your friend throw his life away like that?" His face was suffused with blood, and his words were thrown out with the vigour of a man who knew and loved life. "He knew the curse was real, I saw it on his face." He slumped into the passenger seat, his face distraught. "I should have stopped him. We both should have."

Behind the wheel of my car, I stared unseeingly ahead, not speaking. Eventually I shook my head. "It's not your fault. It's what he wanted. Did you see his face? That's the happiest he's been in a long time." I explained about Ajit's terminal illness and how he knew he hadn't had long to live.

"Cancer or not, why would he waste whatever was remaining of his life like that?"

I smiled sadly. "I don't think you understand, Mark. This is a man whose life has already been wasted. At the very least, he found meaning in his last days. How many of us can hope to say the same?"

—⁓—

According to the day maid who cleaned the house daily, Ajit was found dead in bed the next morning, a smile on his face. His last will and testament named me as executor of his estate—much to my surprise, I was going to say, but the truth is, as I already knew, he hadn't anyone else.

One of the first things I did as executor was to go through his effects and personal property and draw up a list of possessions. I never did find the cello, and it was written off as misplaced.

Or at least that is the official story.

Day after day after day, as I feel the walls of the office close in on me, suffocate me, I take a deep breath and cast my mind afar. In a rented storage space somewhere, there is a beautiful instrument lying in a case, like a beautiful corpse in a coffin, waiting. When one day the end of my life is close at hand—or perhaps sooner, when the daily grind becomes too much to bear—I hope to have the strength, the presence of mind to take out the lovely cello for one last song.

If I'm lucky enough, who knows? Perhaps there will be a little happiness in my song.

THE LEGACY

31 December 2031

Dear Director Lee,

It has been a great honour serving the nation in the Perses program, and I want to take this opportunity to thank you for all the opportunities extended to me during my tenure.

As much as it pains me to do so, the recent chain of events has left me with no choice but to resign my office as Deputy Director (Manned Space Missions). I take full responsibility for the events that have taken place under my watch, and no words can express my sorrow for the deaths of three Singaporean astronauts and heroes, Mr Ethan Mathew, Ms Shazana Rahman and Mr Will Yeo.

The public, at home and abroad, is supremely anxious about the strange circumstances surrounding the incident that occurred on the Martian surface on 21 December 2030, at approximately 13:00 (UTC +8), and understandably so. It is my humble view that they ought to be informed, in adequate detail, of the occurrences on that fateful day, sooner rather than later. To this end, I have prepared a redacted excerpt of the mission report as an appendix to this letter. One of my final acts as Deputy Director would be to urge you, Director, to release the report to the public without delay. It is imperative that the world should know of the truth—as shattering as it might be—in order that we might better prepare for the peril that no doubt now awaits us.

The last day of my tenure will be 30 March 2032. I believe that should leave sufficient time for a successor to be appointed and fully briefed on the situation at hand. In these tumultuous times, I am all too aware of the immense weight that rests on your shoulders, and you have my full assurance that I shall do everything within my power to ensure a smooth transition to my successor.

Yours sincerely,
Mark Fong
Deputy Director (Manned Space Missions)
Singapore Space Exploration Directorate

2.0 Perses Program Overview

The Perses program was founded on 2 February 2025, as a joint initiative between the Republic of Singapore and the United States of America (USA).

Then confronted with a two-theatre war with the Russian Federation and the People's Republic of China, the USA took the decision to partner with an ally sufficiently removed from the hostilities to send the world's first manned spaceflight to the planet Mars. Due to the USA's diversion of strategic assets to the ongoing war effort, it was agreed that mission personnel would be drawn from Singapore.

The program's goal was to land humans on the Martian surface to collect geological data that would determine the feasibility of mining [redacted] deposits. [Redacted] was first discovered on Mars by the rover *Curiosity*, and is a substance that is not known to exist on Earth. Preliminary studies showed that [redacted] possesses [redacted] properties, and it is believed to be [redacted].

* * *

2.6 Perses 6

Final preparations for Perses 6 began shortly after the success of the Perses 5 spaceflight, which all but landed on the Martian surface.

The crew of Perses 6 consisted of Ethan Mathew, Commander; Shazana Rahman, Landing Module Pilot; and Will Yeo, Landing Module Co-pilot.

* * *

5.3 Martian Surface Operations

Shazana, duty pilot at the time, revived the other two crew members from cryogenic-assisted hibernation at 267 elapsed days to make preparations for descent. The landing module was inserted into descent orbit at 270 elapsed days.

37 minutes into powered descent, the landing module was forced to deviate from the planned flight path due to the sudden onset of a severe dust storm. Ground control noted that none of the orbiting or surface probes had picked up any warning signs of the dust storm, which was exceedingly unusual. (Subsequent investigations suggest that freak weather conditions were the likely reason the storm had escaped prior detection.) Shazana took manual control at 40 minutes and manoeuvred the landing

module to approximately 24.5 kilometres north-east of the planned landing site before landing near the foot of *Aeolis Mons*, a mountain situated in the middle of Gale crater. Other than the deviation from the planned descent trajectory and landing site, the landing sequence was routine.

Disembarkation from the landing module began at 272 elapsed days, after the crew had had time to make preparations for surface exploration. After the Martian Roving Vehicle was successfully deployed and tested, the crew mounted the vehicle and drove south for a few minutes before abruptly turning north, towards *Aeolis Mons*, contrary to instructions from mission control. Due to the delay in transmission of radio signals between Mars and Earth, transmissions from the crew were only received after they had dropped out of radio contact, probably due to rock coverage as they entered a cave at the foot of *Aeolis Mons*.

Transcript

Ethan: Mission control, we are deviating from your instructions and heading north instead. It's kind of hard to explain why, but all three of us are, well, experiencing a very strong ... urge to head north. We're going to go with our instincts here, sorry. Over.

[Long silence lasting for about 20 minutes, punctuated only by the occasional cough or murmur.]

Ethan: Mission control, we're nearly at the foot of Aeolis Mons. Something tells me that we are nearly there. We have visual of ... some sort of opening—a cave, it seems. All right, we are dismounting from the Roving Vehicle and proceeding on foot.

[Sounds of equipment clanging, murmured discussions between the crew for a few minutes, which gradually rises to become excited chatter.]

Ethan: [sounding out of breath] Control, you're not going to believe this. We are at the mouth of the cave, and there is some sort of columnar structure on either side of the entrance. We have a strong suspicion that these are not natural formations—

	repeat, NOT natural formations—though we can't be sure, of course. We are going to take a sample.
Shazana:	All right, I've got it.
Ethan:	We're going inside. Wish us luck, ladies and gentlemen.
	[Silence for a few minutes.]
Ethan:	Okay, we are in some sort of long hallway. The longer we look at it, the more it doesn't look naturally formed. It almost looks like a ...
Shazana:	Temple.
Ethan:	Yes, a temple. Or maybe a cathedral. Very high roof. Columns, again, lining the sides. All right, we've reached the end, it seems. There's a small alcove here. Big enough for two, three people maybe. [Whispered discussions.] But with our EVA suits I think we're not going to risk two of us going into such a confined space. Sha, Will—I'm going in.
	[A brief silence, followed by a loud explosion and a heavy thud.]
Will:	What the hell!
Shazana:	Shit, shit! Ethan, you all right? Control, there's been some sort of—well part of the ceiling seems to have caved in, and Ethan's been walled in. There's this

massive stone slab where the entrance to
the alcove was.

Ethan: Sha, Will, do you copy?

Shazana: Copy, we copy. Are you all right?

Ethan: It's a bit tight in here, but I'm okay.

Shazana: What do you see?

Ethan: It's really dark, but ... wait, there's
something glowing.

Shazana: What? [Pause.] Will, did he say glowing?

Will: Yeah, think so.

Shazana: All right, don't move or touch anything.
We'll get you out.

Ethan: It's beautiful. I've never quite seen
anything like it.

Will: Ethan, don't touch anything.

Shazana: What's beautiful?

Ethan: My god.
[Long silence.]

Shazana: Ethan, Ethan, are you okay? [Pause.]
Ethan!

Ethan: [sounding shaken] I'm okay. I'm okay.
Guys, you have to see this. There's this ...
sphere—orb, I think. Glowing. It's really
beautiful. It's in some sort of niche in
the wall.

Will: Ethan, don't touch it.

Ethan: It's perfectly spherical. It's beautiful.
[Pause.] You know what, my friends?

[Pause.] I don't think we are alone in this universe.

[Long silence.]

Shazana: Hang on, let's get you out first.

[Shazana and Will confer in hushed tones.]

Ethan: [whispering] Beautiful.

[He screams.]

Shazana: Ethan! Ethan, what happened?

Will: Shit, shit! [Sounds of pounding.] Fuck, this rock is solid. Sha, we have some explosive charges, right?

Shazana: Yes, but Ethan's too close. He'll be caught in the blast.

Will: We don't have a choice, Sha. He could be dying in there.

Ethan: [in an altered voice] Hola. Nihao. Hello.

Will: What the hell? Ethan, is that you?

Ethan: Your friend is … no longer around, we are afraid.

Will: Who the hell are you?

Ethan: What we have to say, human, is far more important than who we are.

Shazana: What do you want? Please don't hurt him.

Ethan: We have a message for you. For all of you. The time for judgment has come.

Will: Sha, prep the explosive charge. We need to get him out.

Ethan: Your efforts are futile. Listen to what
            we have to say, and your friend will be
            released to you.

Will: Sha? The charge?

Shazana: L-let's just listen first, Will.

Ethan: Very wise. [Pause.] With a story that
            spans aeons, millennia, where to begin?
            [Pause.] We were once like you.
            Humans, as you call yourselves. As our
            civilisation progressed, we sought out
            the stars, as you do now. But there's a
            deadly flaw in our species. You know
            that by now, do you not? The avarice,
            the cruelty. We fought among ourselves
            even as we searched the heavens for
            the sublime, for something that would
            transcend our short, miserable existence.
            A desperate race to find something better,
            before the baseness in us consumed us,
            ripped us apart. [Pause.] But we never
            found it.

            What do you do with something that
            has so much potential, yet is predisposed
            to such selfishness and malice? A seed
            that could spread life to the galaxies, but
            instead leeches off every planet it lands
            on, leaving nothing but an empty husk. Do
            you cage it? Destroy it?

Our civilisation was in its death throes. War, centuries of pointless war, had made sure of that. With our resources almost depleted, we were left with a desperate choice. Preserve a sliver of humanity, or let it flicker out like a candle that had burned on far longer than it should have. The choice ought to have been clear: the universe was better off without us. But we couldn't do it. Whether it was because the instinct of self-preservation is such an inextinguishable urge, or because of some foolish hope that there is, buried deep within humanity, a light that might illuminate the universe for millennia to come—if we could just get it right, somehow.

And so we hoped. We handpicked from humanity at its most innocent—the young—and flung them light years into unknown, unexplored galaxies, onto viable, pristine planets.

And then we died, and you lived. But you were never alone.

Along with each of you, our progeny, we sent humanity's essence, the collective wisdom of the ages, decoupled from corporal form—all contained within this sphere. Through this eye we would watch, only watch, until one day it was time to judge. And the time for judgment has come. You cannot be allowed to live.

Shazana: [in a whisper] My god.

Ethan: Yes, some of you have taken to calling us that. But we are no deity. We are but you, only older. And more wary of what humanity is capable of.

Millennia ago, when you were still in your infancy, we grew concerned about the direction in which you were heading and decided to ... do a reset. Some of your annals remember it as the Great Flood, but for the most part it has receded into the periphery of your consciousness. We had hoped that what remained of you would learn—but no. And this time, the slate will have to be wiped clean, completely clean.

Will: W-what do you mean, wiped clean?

Ethan: This particular experiment has failed. The planet is no longer viable, thanks to you. Judgment has been pronounced, and you are found wanting. All on Earth will be removed from existence.

Shazana: Please, we are trying. Not all of us are the same.

Ethan: Trying? Look at yourselves. Look at
          what you've done to one another, to the
          planet, to the living things entrusted to
          your care. Look at you, the finest and
          bravest humanity has to offer. What
          are you doing here? Are you looking to
          create new worlds, to spread life to the
          universe? No. You're looking for power,
          the power to destroy. Weapons. Oh yes,
          we know why you have come. We have
          been watching, closely. We determined,
          aeons ago, that judgment would be
          pronounced when the experiment
          achieved interplanetary flight, as you
          recently have. Once you were capable of
          spreading beyond your home planet,
          we would have to assess whether you
          were a threat to the rest of the universe.
          And a threat, of course, would have to
          be eliminated.

Shazana: [sobbing] Please, no, no ... At least spare
          our young. [Very softly] Oh, my babies.
          Please ... spare the children.
          [Long silence.]
          Please ...

Ethan: Very well. Let it not be said that we are
          unmerciful. You will be allowed to cull
          from your young the best and brightest,

and they will be sent faraway to another
galaxy, where they will be given another
chance to prove themselves worthy. Just
as we gave you a chance millennia ago.

Shazana: [Sobbing and speaking indistinctly.]
Ethan: But warn your progeny. In the time
you have remaining, warn them. The
same fate awaits all who follow in your
footsteps. There is no other choice.
Until we evolve to weed out the streak
of destruction within us, we are forever
doomed to the same mistakes that
will be the end of us, and everything
around us.

Farewell—we will not speak again. But
in a few millennia, we will do so with your
descendants, perhaps. For their sake, we
hope the outcome will be different.

———

With a sigh, Director Lee threw the sheaf of papers
in his hand onto his desk. Deputy Director Fong was
a good man, but way too naïve. The contents of the
mission report were too explosive to be revealed
to the public. Imagine the chaos, the widespread
panic! As if everyone wasn't edgy enough as it was.
News of the fusillade of asteroids appearing out

of nowhere from the far side of Mars and bearing down towards Earth, likely to hit within weeks; the strange shiny capsules, each the size of a school bus, that had mysteriously emerged from the ground in various cities worldwide, with markings that seemed to indicate they were meant to bear passengers. Rumours floating about—and just how the hell did they hit so close to the truth!—that they were a modern-day Noah's Ark for a doomed planet. The hoi polloi were restive, on the brink of revolt.

And the fool wanted to release the mission report.

He sat up in excitement at the sound of his phone buzzing. Some good news at last, he hoped.

Can confirm 3 seats in Bangkok. Be here by tomorrow evening, no later than 6 p.m. local time.

He leaned back and breathed a sigh of relief. He had started to think that resorting to violence was the only way to secure safe passage for his wife, his son and himself. But Chong always came through.

He closed his eyes and wondered what it would be like boarding one of those strange spaceships. No different from climbing on board one of the last few life boats fleeing the sinking Titanic, no doubt; some guilt, perhaps, but mostly a fierce relief at having been one of those chosen—no, one of those who *fought* for the privilege of surviving. And that privilege had always belonged to the strong.

Darwin would be proud.

He tried, again, to summon up some vestige of guilt, or even pity, but here sheer will and focus, which had served him well throughout his career, failed him.

No matter. A small thrill coursed through him as he imagined being catapulted into space, onto a verdant, pristine planet. He knew that legacies— *dynasties*—were often forged in the fires of chaos.

He couldn't wait.

THE LAST EXORCISM

I must admit, I laughed when James told me he was resigning from his job.

"I didn't know you guys could 'resign'."

He gave a small smile. "It's still a job at the end of the day."

I was tempted to remind him (in jest, of course) of that day, some twenty years ago perhaps, when he told me that he had found his 'calling'. Looking at his weary face, however, I couldn't bring myself to do it. He had been through a lot of late.

"Is it about Mike?" I asked instead.

He bit his lip, face turning sombre.

I felt an uneasiness settle in my stomach. James and his son had been awfully close, and he'd been a wreck after Michael's death. I thought he had finally left all that behind—as best as any parent could leave that sort of thing behind them, of course—but now I wasn't so sure.

He took a long swallow of his whiskey. It was his one weakness, if it even could be considered that.

He was on his second glass, and I'd never known him to take more than three in a night. I glanced at my watch. It was only 8.30 p.m.

I waited. Priest or not, alcohol loosens one's tongue. And clearly he wanted to get something off his chest.

After a minute or two of silence, he spoke.

"What would you do, my friend, if one day you find your fundamental beliefs shattered? Years and years and years, never doubting, never suspecting, not even for a single moment. Then bam!—it all goes out of the window. What then, eh?"

He was talking very quickly, the occasional fleck of whiskey-tinged saliva flying in my direction. When they weren't forming words, his lips hung limply, shining, quivering scarlet flesh. Even when he spoke, it seemed he found the words difficult, like a bucking horse, for the words were clumsy and at times close to unintelligible. I won't deny that at that point I was feeling a bit alarmed, what with what he was saying and the seeming extent to which the liquor had taken root.

"So," I said very cautiously, for I knew not what might set the man off, "you don't believe in God anymore?"

I nearly jumped when he laughed. He laughed and laughed and laughed. I stared, transfixed, and for a few brief moments I considered giving his wife a call, to have him picked up and sent home. But the laughter soon stopped, and he turned to me with startlingly lucid eyes.

"There is a God, Tim. Oh yes, without a doubt, there's definitely one."

His glass was empty. He hailed the waiter and ordered another.

All right, that's the last one, I told myself. *Any more and I'm stepping in.*

"That's the problem of it all, Tim. That's the problem of it all."

"What, that God exists?"

He smiled dryly. "God…and all these beings that exist alongside."

I had heard James's stories before, of course. Exorcisms aren't really that common nowadays, but he had had his fair share. And to be honest they weren't that interesting, really. Not the way James told them. A lot of waiting, then praying, then waiting again. At the risk of sounding extremely insensitive to somebody else's misfortune, the "action" usually lasted for only a very short time, if there was any to begin with.

As if sensing what I was thinking, he said, "I haven't told you an exorcism story for a long time, have I? Truth is, they are more or less the same, all of them. You must know that. I've told you enough."

I nodded.

"But this last exorcism I did, it was different. Not quite a story for bedtime." He laughed with an odd mix of heartiness and shakiness. The pool of amber in his glass was good for just one more swallow, or two at best.

I figured it'd be better to keep him talking. More talking, less drinking. In hindsight I'm not sure that was a good idea. But I couldn't have known.

"Well, it's still quite some time before my bedtime," I said, cracking a wry smile. "Tell me, why don't you."

I had to ask a few more times, but eventually he let it all out.

―――

One day, a member of my congregation approached me. Jane was in her mid-40s, a public relations executive doing rather well in her chosen field.

"It's my husband, Father," she said. She was married to Damien, another member of my congregation. They didn't have any children, so it was always just the two of them coming to Mass, usually arm in arm, smiling.

Forgive me for generalising, but I've always thought public relations people to be a bit...well, long-winded. No fault of theirs, of course, for if it's your job to put a positive spin on things, surely the direct and straightforward answer isn't always the best path to take. But Jane wasn't like that at all, not when she came to me.

"He's been drinking a lot recently. A lot. I think he's been through six Johnnie Walkers the past month. He never used to drink like that, Father. Only after his mother passed away. Then it was like he couldn't stop."

So where did I come in, I asked. Did she think he needed help for alcohol addiction? And for the first time in our conversation, she seemed hesitant.

Quite frankly, I didn't think there was a spiritual dimension to the alcoholism at first. It is true that emotional vulnerability can serve as a foothold for demonic possession, but the majority of alcoholics I've seen in my time suffered from a much more prosaic evil: addiction. But Jane was insistent, and in any case I thought I would take the chance to counsel this wayward member of my flock.

I arrived at the couple's place sometime in the late afternoon. They lived in a five-room flat in the middle of the Ang Mo Kio heartland, a nice spacious apartment with modern décor. I spoke to Damien, who seemed normal enough at first. But a change seemed to come upon him as dusk fell. His manner grew more belligerent, and several times he demanded that I leave. Jane managed to talk him out of it each time, but with increasing difficulty. Finally, I suggested that we pray.

Midway through praying, Damien abruptly stopped and sat up ramrod straight. He glared at me with a hatred that is simply impossible to describe—and that was when I noticed the red glint in his eye. I've told you about that before, haven't I? It's the subtle sort, the kind you have to study carefully to see if it was merely a trick of the light, but in my experience it's the best indication of whether someone has been possessed. It isn't always there, but when the demon is in control, so to speak, it usually is.

He started cursing and swearing at me. First in languages he knew, then in more exotic tongues. Hebrew, for example. That was when I knew, without a doubt, that we were in for a long night. Luckily for all of us, I had come prepared. I flicked holy water at him and chanted the usual prayers.

"What's your name?" I demanded.

"Lilim."

"I command you, unclean spirit, to depart," I began to intone. Rather surprisingly, the demon put up little resistance. There was no screaming, no physical violence. Just a lot of swear words, in a variety of languages. Then, barely ten minutes in, Damien gave a feminine cry and slumped in his seat. And that seemed to be that. I let the man rest and turned to his wife, giving her some instructions on how to tend to her husband for the rest of the night.

I was just about to leave when he stirred.

"You all right, Damien?"

"Fuck you!" he growled, glaring up at me with those unmistakable red-glinting eyes. I have to admit that this time, I was caught completely off guard. I stumbled back and would have probably fallen, if not for the strong hands that caught me.

It was Jane.

"Leave him alone," she hissed, and my heart almost stopped. Her eyes were a horrific red. Not a red gleam, mind you, but actually red—scarlet, in fact. The irises. It is said that this only happens when the demon is really, really pissed, but before that night I'd never witnessed it. I tried to shake myself loose from her grip, but she was strong. Abnormally strong. I began to realise how much trouble I was in. No one knew where I was, and here I was, alone with two demons. I began to fear for my life.

"Who are you!" I yelled at Jane. I had to know who—what I was dealing with.

"I told you. I am Lilim, spirit of the night."

"I already cast you out, demon."

"You did," she sneered, leaning into my face, and it took everything in my being to face that horrifying visage without blacking out. I swear I could feel the very heat of hellfire radiating from her eyes as they drilled into me. "And I climbed into this waiting vessel." She released one hand and patted

her shoulder. I seized the chance. Mustering all the strength I had remaining, I twisted myself free from her grip.

"In the name of Jesus, I claim dominion over you, unclean spirit!"

I must have yelled that at least half a dozen times, just from sheer desperation and terror. God must have sent his guardian angels to be with me that night, for the words seemed to keep her at bay. She screamed and clawed at me, but didn't come any closer.

"What demon claims the body of this child of God?" I demanded, gesturing at Damien.

Jane—or Lilim, I mean—stopped her growling momentarily. "He is my son."

She must have noticed my surprise, for she gave a low chuckle. "Yes, the ability to multiply is not something that is bestowed upon humans alone." She paused and seemed to study my face for a while. "I sense…pain. Ah, you are a father, are you not?"

I willed myself to remained expressionless. If they knew about Mike, they would pounce on it. Emotional vulnerability is a demon's favourite snack.

"Ah, more pain still. An illness, perhaps. Or maybe even death?"

"Shut your trap, demon." The words escaped before I could even stop myself.

Her eyes blazed brighter. "Ah, there is something familiar about you. Could it be… Oh my, surely not."

"What?" I snapped.

"I thought I'd come across someone like you before—while I was still languishing in Hell, I mean. The likeness in demeanour and speech...amazing. Chip off the old block, as they say."

"What are you saying?" I could barely hear myself. I didn't want to hear anymore, but I had to. I had to know.

"You know very well what I mean, human. I've met your son. Somewhere you're praying he wouldn't be."

"Mike was a saint!" I screamed. I spat and cursed in her face. "How dare you!"

"Your God works in very mysterious ways," she sneered.

"Liar. You are the spawn of the Father of Lies, and lying is your very nature."

"Is that so, human? You don't sound so sure." She leaned in, as far as she could. "Shall I tell you what I know about him?"

And she proceeded to tell me Mike's deepest, darkest secrets and fears. Some I knew, some I didn't. But I knew at once that she was telling the truth.

I was weeping now. But I had to do my duty, all the same. Forcing Mike's face from my mind, I began chanting.

"Stop!" she screamed. "After what I've told you, you dare banish me to whence I came? Do you know what I can do to your son when I return?"

I continued through gritted teeth. I could taste the saltiness of tears in my mouth. I could feel the burning in my chest. The buzz in my ears. Most of all—the pain, the fear in my heart.

My little Mikey...barely on the cusp of adulthood when he died. What could he have done to deserve this? How could any child deserve this?

The demon screamed again. There was a certain ring of desperation now. And—strange as it might sound—a sliver of sorrow. She leaned in again, and something I saw in those terrifying eyes made me stop chanting. What did I see? I'm not quite sure I know it myself. It was unbelievable. Unbelievable. Even if I told you, I don't think you would believe me.

"Spare my son," she rasped. "Banish me if you will, but spare him. I beg of you." Her eyes held mine, and for the life of me, I just couldn't tear my gaze away. "You are a father...you must know my pain. Spare him."

"That's it?" I said, when it was clear that James had stopped his narrative.

"That's it."

"So what did you do?" It was not like James to leave his listener hanging.

"I did what I had to." His voice was suddenly hard. "What choice was there?"

"James," I said softly. "Demons lie, you know that. You tell me that all the time. I'm sure Mike—"

"Don't!" he almost spat out. "Don't, please."

I stared at the table. I didn't know where to look, what to say. I was grateful when he finally broke the silence—until I heard what he had to say, that is.

"You want to know what I did? I made a deal." He gave a dry laugh. "A deal with a demon. Most unbecoming of a priest, eh?"

I licked my dry lips nervously. "D-deal?"

"Yes. What would you have me do? God had abandoned me. God had condemned my only son." He glared at me—then with a frightening suddenness, he banged the table with his fists. *"What would you have me do!"*

"James…" I muttered, holding out a hand—to soothe my friend, or for my own protection, I don't know. "You did what you had to, I know."

The fury had left his eyes, leaving them hollow. "I banished her…but spared her son, like she asked." His voice was flat, devoid of all emotion. "In return… in return, she was to be…*kind*—" a tear rolled down his cheek "—to Mikey."

I think we would have sat there the entire night if the bar hadn't had to close. Towards the end he was almost comatose, eyes open but unseeing, the ghosts of words, inaudible, twitching on his lips. Eventually I paid the bill, swung his arm over my shoulder and half-dragged him out of the bar.

A thought struck me at the door.

"What do you mean, you spared the son? You told me before that demons can't stay on the earthly plane for long without a vessel. You didn't leave him in the husband—Damien—did you?"

I turned around to face him, but he was hunched over, and I only saw his mussed-up hair. For some reason, a queasy fear was starting to fill my stomach, and a desperate urgency pressed me. I shook him. "James, dammit, answer me!"

I stared at him for a few more seconds, and was just about to give up when he started to raise his head slowly.

"James, what did y—"

My voice withered. His eyes, gleaming red, met mine, and a slow smile began spreading across his lips.

ABOUT THE AUTHOR

S.J. Huang previously worked as legal counsel before leaving the field to pursue other interests, among them fiction writing. *The New Singapore Horror Collection* is his first published work. Whodunnits and psychological thrillers are his guilty pleasures, and his one regret is having devoured all of Agatha Christie's books far too quickly. He can be contacted at huang.sj@yahoo.com.